THE NIGHT PRINCE
&
THE ROSEFINCH

THE FIRST BODY

AUTHOR'S NOTE

A good story is only one part of a truly good book, and this book was shaped by many different hands. Much like any ancient, mythological tale passed down, remixed, forgotten and resurrected through the centuries, this book is a tapestry of several different artists, several different points of inspiration, and several different interpretations.

The versions of the characters that you craft in your mind while reading are just as powerful as the illustrated versions of them in this book. As creator, I do not seek to defend or deny any one icon that emerges from this story, but rather, I invite every iteration to join in on the feast.

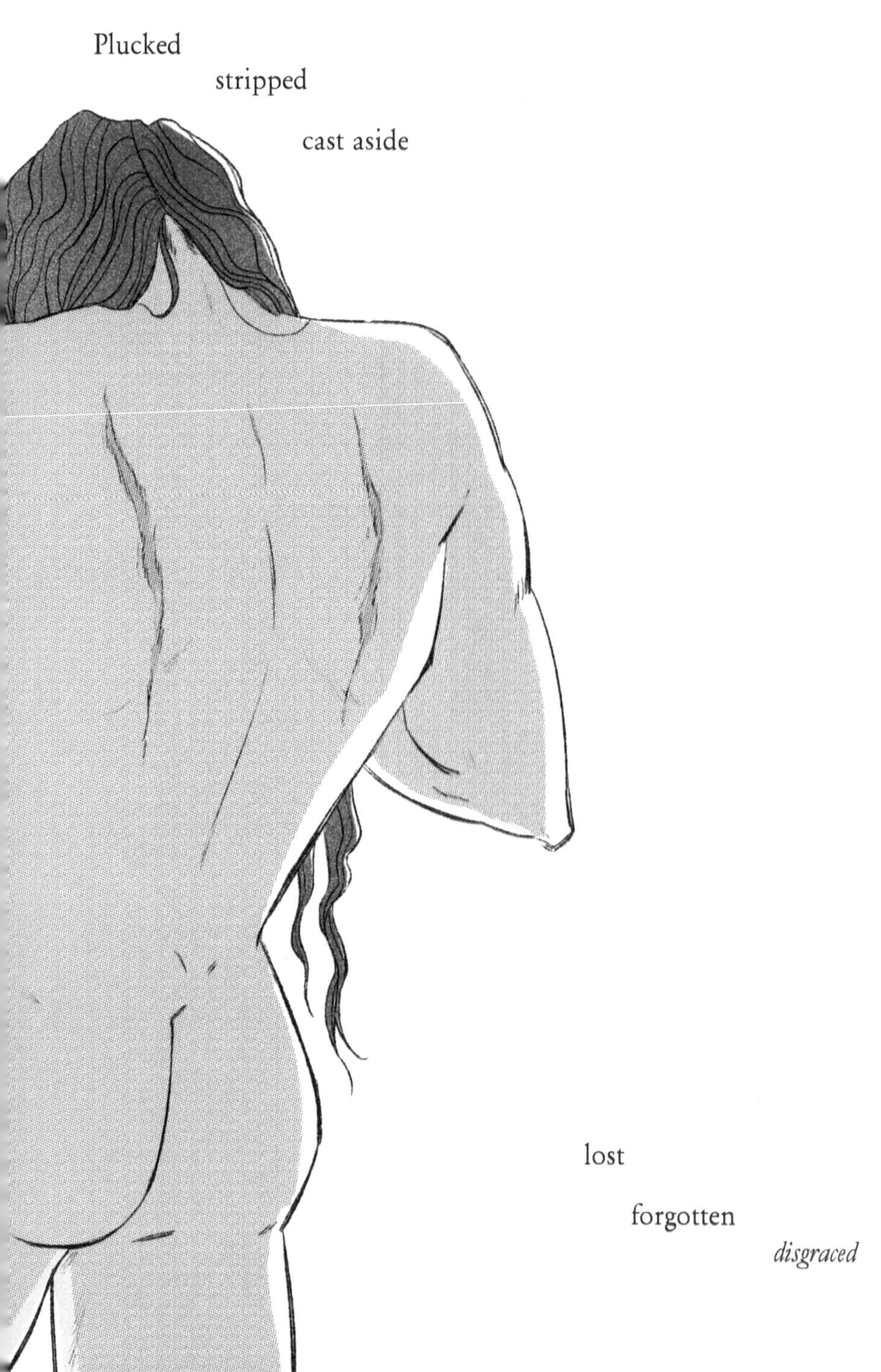

Plucked

stripped

cast aside

lost

forgotten

disgraced

THE VOW

SOMETIME DURING THE LONG FALL, HE LOSES consciousness. At first, the world is cold, the wind icy, and his body frigid. When he wakes up, the world is hot. The humidity seeps into his clothes, sticking to him with every movement. He hauls himself off the ground just to stop his own limbs from touching.

He finds himself in a dark, unfamiliar city. The sky is black with no stars, and the closest light is anchored to a wall above a metal door. Two men stand on either side of it, leering at the newcomer with blatant curiosity. They wear heavy, dark clothes, seemingly unaffected by the miserable heat of this place. If not for the sky, this place could be mistaken for a human city.

"Look at that. Haven't seen one out here in ages."

"Mm, must have had a long trip down."

"Precious little thing. Looks like he needs a hand."

The *little thing's* white clothes stick out so plainly as the other two men in scant, dark uniform approach him. Even though his layers are strangling him in this heat, he refuses to take anything off as the hulking figures guarding the door loom over him.

"Hey beautiful." The guard with a black ring through his septum gives a smile. "You all alone?"

The being in white hugs his arms to his chest and musters up a determined expression. "I-I need a guardian."

"I'll be your guardian." The other one with a rocky pauldron on his left shoulder smirks. "I'll always come when you call."

They snicker at the creature in white. He holds his ground.

"I'm here to summon a guardian. The *proper* way." The unwelcome stranger enunciates to the guards.

Both of them frown back.

"No one who comes down this way's any fuckin' fun." The one with the nose ring huffs and stalks back to the door, fishing in his shirt for a key. A thin black tail swings at his back.

"You sure about this?" Pauldron asks, eyeing the creature, freshly fallen. "You'll have a much easier time out here with us."

"I know what I'm doing," the fallen in white says, though his voice barely leaves him—not enough tinder for the flint.

The guards exchange glances, and Pauldron mutters, "We don't call them *guardians*."

Nose Ring unlocks the door as the fallen approaches. There is no room visible on the other side, only a wall of pitch black. The fallen in white narrows his eyes, trying to discern anything useful in the dark, until he feels two hands placed onto his back.

"Don't say we didn't warn you." A voice purrs in his ears before he is shoved beyond the threshold and into the darkness.

It doesn't just steal his sight, but all of his senses. He stumbles into something hard and warm, bouncing off it and into a wall, where he tries to catch himself, only to be shoved forward again by unseen hands. They are all around him, bodies much larger than his own, flowing forward toward something unseen. Vague shapes begin to emerge out of the dark, but not fast enough to stop him from getting his legs taken out from under him.

He collides fully into someone's jacket, much too slow to stop them from grabbing him by his tangled mess of hair.

"What's this?"

Faces clarify from within the shadow, and the creature in white can no longer pretend that these pierced, inked, clawed, and tusked people are anything other than demons.

"He pushed you," one of the demons says, lips pulling into a tusked smile. "He should apologize."

The hand in his hair tightens as the other one flicks a forked tongue. "He looks like he came from upstairs."

"Not sure." Tusks gives him an appraising look. "Hard to tell with all those clothes on."

"Let's give him a hand." The demon with their hand in the creature's hair yanks harder, and the one with tusks grabs the back of that sticky white shirt.

The creature struggles, trying to twist out of the demon's grasp and only managing to make it worse. His eyes are finally adjusting to the crushing darkness, and he can see he is surrounded by bodies on all sides. They have him cornered in some kind of large room with demons packed in wall-to-wall. Sweat streaks his skin as another demon swoops in to grab him by the throat. His white top pulls tighter and tighter *and tighter* until the hot air rushes over his bare skin and the creature goes stiff.

Every demon in the room can see the two parallel red gouges running down his back. The wounds do not bleed anymore, but they are an angry, weeping red. They are savage wounds with a finality that everyone in the room understands at once. The demon with tusks admires his own work as he pushes aside the fabric of the fallen angel's torn uniform.

"I'm here for a ritual!" The fallen struggles to get his voice heard with the hand around his throat. "I must take a vow."

"What do you need that for?" The demon loosens his grip from a clenching tightness, to a soft brush of fingertips. "I'll be your bond."

"I know how it works," the fallen says back, voice shaking in the presence of these demons in their own home. "You cannot deny me. I've come for a ritual, and I'll have it."

The demon looks around him at the gathered crowd, gesturing out at everyone with a smirk. "Why go through all that trouble? Just pick one of us and you won't have to roll the dice."

"You could even have a couple of us," another whispers from behind, long fingers brushing over his wind-swept nest of hair. "If you wanted a really nice time."

Gooseflesh ripples over the fallen's arms, but he shakes his head as if to wake himself and his hands ball into fists.

"I invoke my right to a binding ritual."

Smoke curls around the fallen's feet, rushing up from the floor and condensing beside him into the shape of another demon, this one with a polearm held firm at her side.

"You heard him," she says, monotone and steady in the face of the leering crowd. She waves her hand and all of the other demons take a step away from the fallen with sighs.

"This way," the demon with the polearm says, catching the fallen's eye. "You asked for a vow. You'll have it."

She turns away, taking a brisk pace and parting the sea of onlookers. The fallen startles after her, taking nervous glances at all the eyes glued to him. His guide escorts him through the dim room, and at last, the fallen takes note of the music pulsing around him. There are drinks in these demons's hands. They appear to be cutting through some kind of club, though his guide looks none too impressed.

Down a few flights of stairs, around a couple of sharp turns, and the fallen sees an open door leading to a long, narrow stone bridge. The surface is barely big enough for the two demons currently grappling each other on top of it, and the fallen stiffens as one of them pins the other to the floor, pushing them both dangerously close to the edge. The heat down here is far worse, shimmering in the air, causing the fallen begins to pant. Another demon with a polearm guards the open entrance, and they give the fallen a stern look before nodding at their compatriot and walking out onto the bridge where the two demons are snarling and snapping at each other.

"Demons!" The second guard shouts into the cavernous pass. Everyone goes still, including the two combatants currently half wrapped around each other, jaws in one another other's skin.

"We have a ritual! Clear the pass!"

The two brawlers jump to their feet, glancing at each other warily before sprinting to the other side of the stone bridge to rejoin the stands full of spectators. A hush settles over the crowd, and the guard comes back to take their place beside their companion.

"Go on, then," the guard says to the fallen. "Your demon awaits."

The fallen looks between the two of them, dressed in far less modern clothing than the demons in the club, and walks through the archway. As he slowly inches forward, he raises his hand to cover his eyes from the blinding glow of boiling magma flowing beneath him. A burning river runs just under the narrow stone bridge he now walks on, one wrong step away from a swift death. He can hardly think straight from all this heat, but the rest of the world can see him painfully clear.

A reed of an angel is catching his breath over the Great River, puny compared to all the proper demons gathered. His torn white uniform reveals the unmistakable mark of disgrace. He looks freshly fallen, all dazed and confused, battered by his one-way trip. All the more exciting, the demons whisper to each other from the stands carved into the walls, to see this precious thing out here, summoning up its courage in front of a full coliseum crowd.

Who is this fallen angel that interrupted their brawl?

"He looks like he just got here."

"Did he know about this before he fell?"

"What could he have done? Little thing like him."

"Who will he catch?"

The fallen turns to take stock of the crowd of betting demons, no doubt attempting to predict who will show.

"Does anyone have a knife?" The fallen reaches a shaky hand out toward the stands, as if any of them are close enough to give it to him. The bridge is far too long.

He twitches at the sound of something sliding across stone, and turns toward the demon who escorted him as she points at a knife on the ground. Wasting no time, he snatches the blade up and brings the edge to his palm. There is a single second of hesitation, looking at his unbroken skin, before he slices his own hand open and holds it out over the river.

The crowd is murmuring with a fervor now.

"He didn't think twice."

"He knows what he's doing."

"Hah! Not so puny after all!"

The fallen's arms drop to his side like he's finally let go of something impossibly heavy. His body sways, legs on the verge of giving out, and the crowd slowly goes quiet as they all wait for a sign of movement in the molten river.

The guards whisper to one another.

"Silence is deafening," the heavier guard murmurs.

Their companion quirks her brow. "Maybe his is already dead."

"This one looks like he knows something. Knowledge is dangerous upstairs."

The fallen's escort rests her arm on her partner's shoulder. "He either broke a very small rule, or."

They look at each other and snicker.

"You think he hooked a big one?"

"Might explain the delay."

The fallen can't keep himself standing. He sinks to his knees—a ragged mess of tattered clothing, sweat-streaked bronze skin, and unkempt hair—here over the Great River of Hell, and puts his hands together in prayer.

The demons begin to laugh at this desperate gesture. He *must* be new to do something like this. Doesn't he know that prayers won't be answered down here? The crowd is hungry to see him met by a cruel master, or better yet, a pathetic one. After all, it is the size and breadth of one's disgrace that acts as the bait to lure in a demon.

The laughter goes on just a little too long, confusion and annoyance seeping in to take its place. The ritual never takes this much time. The guards should throw him into the river and be done with it. Whispers and jeers grow louder until they are shouts and heckles, but the guards pay them no mind. They are watching the magma, the way it glows and bubbles, and of course, the way the fallen angel mutters into his interlocked hands.

He is not praying. The angel whispers, "please," over and over again—a spool of pretty thread unraveling before a hungry crowd. More curious onlookers have joined the swelling crowd, until the room is full of steam and tension.

"Toss him in the river!"

Someone shouts and the energy of the room snaps into a frenzy. Gambling is fun, but destruction even better, and it's the only thing left that would justify the interruption to their scheduled bloodbath. They are all fixed on the pathetic creature in white, so the guards see the swell in the river first—something so large that it disturbs the never-ending flow of magma streaming down the river, sending fiery rivulets spilling onto the cracked banks.

When the surface breaks, the crowd howls. A shower of magma bursts onto the rocks around them, but just as quickly as their excitement peaks, the crowd falls silent as a demon rises taller and taller and *taller* from the river. Gray, membranous wings unfurl from his back, spanning the width of the crevasse. The demon shakes stray embers and cooling rock from his body, taking in his surroundings with narrowed eyes visible beneath the full suit of rocky armor.

The guards on the bridge drop into sweeping bows, and the crowd follows suit until the entire room is bent in half before the sight of this massive demon. The stands are far from silent by now. The whispers rise up through the steam.

"Which one is it?"

"How is this possible?"

"Is that the Night Prince?"

"What in the world did that little whelp do?"

The demon gives a displeased look at the speck in white kneeling on the bridge before him. With a huff, he leans down closer, settling his hands on either side of the fallen angel who summoned him. The fallen's hands are still dripping with the blood he used to call this Prince to him as he kneels there, shivering.

"What do you want?"

The demon's head is as long as the fallen angel is tall. His voice is the sound of a hungry fire, or a thousand beating wings. It rushes through the room, filling every corner with his impatience. His face is half-hidden by a mask of carved stone, wet black eyes reflecting the fallen's disheveled appearance back at him.

"Y..." The fallen's voice catches on his dry throat and he has to muster up spit just to speak. "You came because I bled into the river."

The demon does not look impressed.

"We're supposed to help each other." The fallen angel staggers back to his feet, reaching dumbly toward the demon's massive face. "Please, I-I won't ask much. I just need somewhere to go and I'll—"

"No." The demon speaks plainly, stealing any more words right out of the air.

The fallen's eyes fly open. "What?"

"I'm a Prince of the underworld. I have no time for this. Why in the world should I care what happens to you?"

The fallen's shoulders sag, completely unprepared for the possibility of something as simple as refusal.

"But, there is an accord! It's law, it can't be broken. The ritual is complete, my pain is your pain, if I die then you—"

The great demon Prince throws his head back and laughs, igniting the crowd back to life with him. "Do you honestly believe that if I crushed you like a bug here and now that it would be enough to kill me? I'll need more convincing beyond laws and rituals from one who has broken his own oath."

Stunned and panting, the fallen angel looks as though a stiff wind would knock him off his feet. His eyes are verging on wild as he swallows more steam, and now it is the crowd holding their breath in anticipation of the rebuttal, or the crushing.

Shaking his head, the fallen gives the slightest of shrugs. "I'll do anything." His voice is a mouse's squeak.

The demon's eyes widen beneath the mask of stone. "Anything?"

The angel nods in affirmation, and the demon's rocky armor *cracks*. The tension in the air snaps as the gathered hoard is there to witness the end of the angel's long fall.

"Anything?" The demon Prince sounds delighted as he lifts his left hand off the bridge and makes a fist.

The fallen startles as chunks of rock break apart, revealing a huge clawed hand of gray flesh and fur. The demon flicks the loose stone shards away before he reaches toward the fallen's legs. The instinct to run clenches through the fallen's limbs, but resignation is on its heels, and he lets the demon slide a finger as thick as a tree trunk between his thighs. His white skirt bunches up around the demon's skin, and the fallen turns his face from the lewd sight, completely unprepared for the warmth of living skin pressed up against the center of his body. As the demon lifts him up off the ground, the fallen startles forward to grip the demon's thick palm to keep from losing his balance.

"How does it feel to be so high up without your wings?" The demon's rumbling laugh is underscored by more cracking rock. All of his armor is peeling away like eggshell as he holds his hand up to his face to examine the flightless bird perched on his finger.

The fallen shifts his legs, his face flushed with heat and shame at the demon's warm finger between his thighs.

"Does it tremble at the fear of heights?" the demon ponders as the crowd cheers.

Shoulders hunched, the fallen bows his head, hiding behind a mess of tangled dark hair.

"The little angel says he will do anything!" The demon's voice effortlessly fills the cavern. "What shall we start with?"

When the last of the rock armor falls away, the demon Prince stands tall in all his inhuman glory. Pale white fur covers his chest, puffed with the pride of a fisherman displaying his rare catch. He stands as a blend of human and animal, and the fallen angel's eyes struggle to focus on him as he preens before his audience.

"You're lucky," the demon says to his flightless bird. "I've been away for some time. I could use a warm welcome."

His is the smile of a hungry man smeared across a bat's muzzle. The fallen opens his mouth but all the words have burned away in this heat. With a tilt of the demon's wrist, the fallen spills into his large, leathery palm. Head still spinning, the little bird yelps at the sudden weight of the demon's tongue. He is plastered to the demon's thick skin with hot saliva as the crowd roars below.

"This is a far better reception than I could have ever hoped for," the demon says. "It won't be long at all before you taste like one of us, but I'll enjoy this wine while it lasts."

The demon turns away from the Great Bridge, wings gone taut, his new pet held tight in his hand. Hardly any time to fear for his life, the angel only closes his eyes as they quickly set off through the unbearable heat. It's a shock when nothing burns his skin, or even touches it at all. His body is cased in stone, too dark to see, entirely at the mercy of the demon Prince who holds him like a child holds a toy.

The fallen angel goes slack with relief.

When next he sees light, his eyes burn from the glow of torches instead of magma. Before his vision has time to adjust, he is pulled by the arm into a hallway where the impossible heat dies down. Wherever they are, the walls are a mere blur as they move so quickly, the fallen can't see a single detail. He hardly feels like he's moving at all, until they come to such an abrupt stop, he nearly loses his balance. The sight of a cavernous room full of softly running water is enough to steady him, until his guide slips an arm around the fallen's back, crushing their chests together.

This Prince of demons now looks like a man, though the edges of his smile still play at something wilder. Streams of corn silk hair seem to move all their own, framing the Prince's ethereal face. He holds his prize by the waist as he pulls the tattered strips of the ruined white uniform from lean, warm shoulders. The Prince wears no clothes, and the fallen burns where the demon's hips touch the front of his skirts, even with the chill of his moon-touched skin. He looks carved from its very surface—unnaturally bright and uncomfortably close.

"I haven't seen these clothes in a very long time," the demon says.

His eyes now shine with mischief as the angel watches his teeth—just a little too big, a little too sharp.

"That is a very long way to fall without wings. Tell me what you did. What sin is so great and terrible that it pulled me all the way from the world of humans?"

The flightless bird turns his head away. "It doesn't matter what I did."

The demon only smiles wider as his fingers slide down the twin scars on the angel's back. "I'm not just any demon, you know?"

The fallen angel shivers at the demon's fingers now tracing the gouges on his back. The demon grows harder against him, the shape of his body pronouncing itself against the angel's while he murmurs.

Pressing his mouth to the angel's ear, the demon whispers in a husky voice, "You have the great fortune of falling into the hands of the Night Prince."

The angel's eyes widen, breath catching at the strong scent of woodsmoke pouring off the demon's skin.

"Do you know what they usually do to welcome me home after such a long time in the human world?"

Shaking his head, the angel closes his eyes as if that will calm some of the heat bellowing in the demon's voice. All the darkness really does is heighten the sensation of the demon's hands roaming down his back and over the fabric of his skirt.

"It usually takes at least three others to warm me again. And this was a rather *unusual* occasion."

The Pale Prince of Night slips his hand between his wingless finch's thighs. The demon appears to be arousing himself on words alone, and the angel clenches his hands into fists, afraid to move his own hips and invite by mistake.

"Tell me what you did, and I will go easy on you."

The demon's breath carries the nip of frost, his body the heat of burning wood.

The angel opens his mouth, bracing at the fingers pulling up the edge of his skirt. He is trembling with some great effort as the Night Prince touches his thighs. His eyes are watering as if the scent of smoke is enough to burn him. With a snap of teeth, the angel shuts his mouth again, pressing his pursed lips to the demon's shoulder to signify his refusal.

"Little rosefinch with his wings plucked off." The Night Prince speaks low with his hands groping underneath the angel's skirt. "Let's see if you satisfy."

With dizzying quickness, the demon spins the angel away from him and marches him toward the steps into the basin of water. It is a beautiful bath of clear running water that flows from one end of the room, disappearing underneath a ledge on the other side. As the angel glances at a mural of black and blue tiles on the ceiling, the Night Prince yanks his skirt down his thighs.

Clapping his hand over his mouth, embarrassed heat floods the angel's skin. The Night Prince curls his fingers around the angel's hips, and the angel startles at the press of hardened flesh against his back.

"Are you untouched?" the Prince murmurs in the angel's ear. "Or is that what got you clipped?"

Some ember of dignity flares to life as the angel lifts his chin up. "No."

"Good."

The Night Prince sighs warm smoke against the angel's ear and begins to push him into the water. The angel's breath comes faster with every step into the bath. He's waist deep when the Night Prince pulls his hands away and gives a short whistle.

Scaled faces emerge from the clear bath water, hands reaching out for the angel as he stumbles away—only to back up into another body. A trio of beautiful, horse-haired selkies slide their silken hands across the angel's shoulders. Turning to look behind him, he sees two more with their arms wrapped around the Night Prince's waist, sunless fingers playing with the curls of colorless hair trailing down the demon's abdomen.

"My Prince," one of them sighs. "You were gone for so long."

"We had no work."

"We nearly died of boredom."

The angel stiffens as the selkies play with his own bedraggled nest of hair.

"I'm sorry I was away," the Night Prince coos back at them. "But I'm home now."

"With quite the prize." The nearest selkie turns the angel's face toward theirs, smiling sweetly around needle teeth. "Where did you find it?"

"He found me," the Night Prince declares, staring at the angel's face until the intensity of his gaze forces the angel to look away. "He's my reward after a long journey. Prepare him for me, but don't get carried away. He's untouched. Keep him that way."

"Yes, my Prince."

With six hands roaming all over his body, the angel can hardly think straight. He twitches and jumps at each new point of contact, burning from the inside out as the Night Prince watches him with the same misshapen smile. When the selkies drag the angel underwater to wash his waves of loose curls, he almost forgets to hold his breath.

The selkies whisper to him beneath the surface.

Lucky boy.

Our Prince is the most handsome.

We'll take your place if you don't want him.

He gasps as they let him above water again, and yelps when he feels glossy fingers brushing over the seam at the center of his body. Attempting to pull away only snares him in the selkies' grip, like seaweed clinging to his skin. Two of them hold his hands and arms in place as the third traces over the slight lip of hairless bronze skin between his thighs. The angel grits his teeth, turning his head away even though he can't escape the weight of the Prince's gaze on him.

"He may not be enough for you, my Prince," the selkie laments with their fingers pressing against hot skin. The angel can't breathe with these untouched parts of him getting cataloged like cuts of meat.

"He won't open," the selkie diagnoses.

The Prince grins as the other two selkies comb their fingers through his hair. "Not for you. You're not the one he summoned."

With a sigh, the selkie slips their hand down lower, washing every inch of skin they can find until they're satisfied and the angel is completely flushed.

"Your prize is ready, my Prince."

All five of the selkies sink back into the water, seemingly dissolving into it until they're gone from sight. The angel shivers as he scans the suddenly clear bath.

"Are they always here or do they come and go?" he asks, nervously shifting his feet over the tile.

With no sound nor visible movement, the Night Prince once again appears an inch away from the angel to slip his hands around the angel's waist.

"Is that really what you want to ask me?"

Eyes flashing open, the angel shies away with his hands braced on the demon's chest.

"I'll give you one question before I take you," the Prince says. "Make it count."

Words are failing him once again as the angel feels taut skin nestling between his thighs. He doesn't go tense the way he did when the selkies touched him though. An entirely new emotion rips through him as he feels his body responding to a language he's never spoken before. Something about this demon is changing the very fabric of his skin.

"What's happening?" His voice comes out in a hush as he stares between their bodies, their mismatched skin meeting in the water.

The demon's hand closes around the back of the angel's neck, drawing their gazes together again. His cock burns between the angel's thighs and an utterly alien softness spirals out from inside a place he thought hollow.

"This is the ritual you demanded. The accord between our worlds that you hold so high."

The Night Prince drags his hand down the front of the angel's neck, thumbing at the brown bead of his nipple until the angel's entire chest stipples with sensation.

"Your pain is my pain," the demon says. "My pleasure is your pleasure. Whether you want it or not."

The angel gasps at the strong, new heat searing down his chest as the Night Prince admires the sight with heavily lidded eyes.

"There is a reason your precious gods don't tell you about this agreement. It's a gamble, after all, to tie yourself to one of us."

With a slight pinch of the demon's fingers, the angel digs his nails into pale skin, trying and failing to swallow a groan. His hips feel like they're blooming into something completely new as his chest reacts to a sensation he has never been given before.

"Not all of my kin are so generous. You are very lucky indeed, little wingless rosefinch."

With a flash of white teeth, the room grows dim around them. The Night Prince hauls the angel out of the water, holding him tight to his chest as the wash room goes completely dark. Cool wind howls in the angel's ears, rushing over his entire body and drying the water from his skin and hair. Every movement is disorienting and he has no choice but to cling to the Prince's shoulders as the two of them silently move through the halls of the Night Palace.

The angel's head spins as he is dropped onto the plush cover of a bed, but when he tries to scramble away, strong hands snap tight around each of his ankles. The Night Prince pulls the angel's hips closer, winding his pale arms around trembling thighs.

"Oh, you must have done something terrible up there," the Prince sighs against the closed folds of skin between the angel's legs.

The angel twitches at the hush of warm breath.

"Was that the most you've ever been touched?" the Prince asks, brushing his own pink lips against the slowly darkening seam of the angel's body.

The angel's hips jump when the demon licks him, and he feels the hot rushing water of the bath once again, only it's inside him this time, churning through him as his body begins to open up like the petals of a flower. Another pass of the Night Prince's long tongue, and something emerges from inside the angel's body to meet the demon's touch.

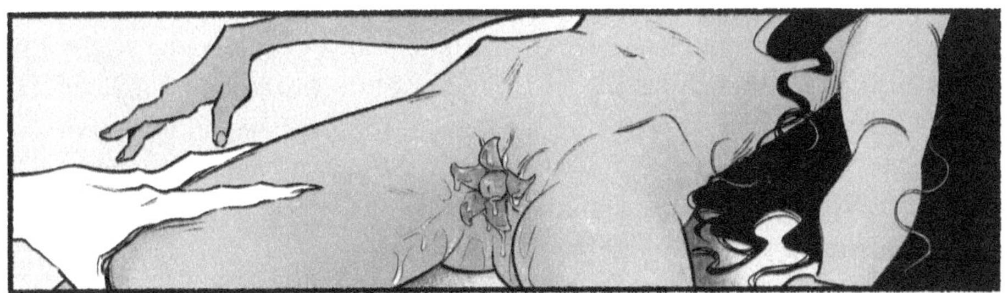

The angel shouts like he's been wounded, knees shaking as the Night Prince licks him open, recklessly coaxing out brand new skin. The moment there's room for it, the Prince closes his mouth around the head of the angel's untouched cock.

Back arching, the angel bites his own lip to bleeding and it's still not enough to stop him from shouting as the Night Prince sucks the stem of the angel's cock into his mouth. Countless new nerves sing against the pressure of a thick tongue and the strange vulnerability of his body being held open. An entire new system is laid bare to be exploited by this demon and it robs the angel of his thoughts. His flesh caught in the jaws of a hungry beast, the warm air on all this new, slick skin—it's too much to bear. Just as he thinks to cover his own eyes, the light in the room flickers and he is once again plunged into complete darkness.

The Night Prince pulls his mouth free just to slip his tongue all the way down into the uncharted hollows of his bird.

"No!"

The flightless rosefinch is suspended in endless night, his body intent on betraying him as the demon savors the taste of his cunt. It should hurt, it should burn, it should sicken him to his core, and yet this body that was sacred a few hours before now asks for something new. His eyes can't see, his wings can't flutter, and his hips are filling up with an all-consuming heat that aches for release. The deeper the Night Prince slides his tongue inside of him, the worse it gets. This demon is unearthing entire passages that he didn't know he had tucked inside him, and with every nerve ending carelessly awoken, his panic swells.

"P...Poison!" the angel chirps against his own fingers. That tongue could be anywhere inside him. He can't see but it feels as though it hasn't stopped snaking deeper into his body.

"There is poison! Get it out!"

Invisible hands push his legs apart, and the angel keens as the Night Prince finds something electric buried within him—something so devious and wicked it gives him the flesh of a mortal man. Sweat beads along the angel's brow as his cock throbs without attention. There are terrible things rooted inside him and they need to come out.

He tries to move his legs, and the Prince lets go of him, graciously allowing the angel to spread his knees even further apart. It's all the angel can do to hurry this process along. He certainly doesn't know how to do this himself, and he keeps his hands firmly buried in the sheets beneath his body.

The Night Prince retracts his tongue, and the angel tears at the bedding from the slow slide against his walls, but it's not enough. He pushes his hips up, a single drop of fluid dripping down the length of his cock. When the Night Prince licks the droplet away, the angel grits his teeth with a whine.

"Everyone loves to brag about how good fallen angels taste." The Prince sighs. "I didn't believe them before today."

Weak as he is, the angel still tries to brace his feet on the bed so he can pick his hips up higher, displaying his desperation.

"Oh?" The demon's voice is all around him, rushing through the dark, slipping down his ear canals. "Has he decided he enjoys being ruined?"

Taut skin presses in tight against the slit of the angel's cunt and his body reacts with a violent need. He can't explain how he knows that this is what will cleanse him. He can only whimper as he waits, legs trembling, unable to initiate or deny.

The angel's teeth chatter with woodsmoke filling his nose again. He still can't see a damned thing, but the demon's long hair brushes over his chest, his body splitting open like overripe fruit as the demon eases the head of his cock to fill him again.

The Night Prince groans in the angel's ear. "Even better than a human..."

The demon's body is taking shape around the angel's as he moves inside the space he carved for himself. This is what the angel needed. This is how he'll get the poison out. The rot is beginning to wither with the Night Prince bending around him, sinking deeper. The angel's cock aches the way his back once did right before he sprouted his wings. If only someone would touch him, loosen the cap, get this acid out so he can breathe again. He's full to bursting, the Night Prince pushing him to insanity as he pulls their hips flush.

The angel is choking. He's never even imagined a violation like this—a pressure so wild, the unbearable fullness, and worst of all, the way he needs more of it, as much as he can get. Tears spring to his eyes when the Night Prince jerks his hips. He lets out a sob when the Night Prince grabs his waist and does it again. After that, he doesn't have room in his head to count every thrust.

Slowly, the light in the room sparks back to life. A soft white glow spills over the angel's body. He can see exactly how the Pale Prince of Night has taken him—his legs so shamelessly twined around the demon's torso. The angel is entranced by the look of hedonistic pleasure smeared on a face far more handsome than a demon has the right to be.

If not for his manners, and his actions, and his words, the Night Prince would be truly beautiful. With his teeth bared and his lip curled in pleasure, the angel doesn't see beauty. He sees the reddened tip of his own hard cock and he throws his head back.

The Night Prince moans, and something unfurls inside the angel, stretching him open even more. The angel's vision goes red and he finally starts to come apart, all the heat of the underworld splashing onto his stomach in bursts. Weakness seizes him, his body going slack as the Night Prince holds his hips up off the bed to keep fucking him. The angel's eyes roll shut as the poison leaves him, wave after wave, taking all his strength with it. It doesn't seem right, that there should be so much fluid in him, but it doesn't stop even when he goes limp.

If the Prince notices the angel losing consciousness, he doesn't show it. He can't stop moving once his cock takes root. Minutes spiral into hours in a haze, time slipping away as he starts to fill the angel with all his pent-up heat. His very skin changes shape once or twice, and the angel wakes back up with a sharp startle and another violent spill onto his own chest. He smells like summer heat and fresh rose blossoms.

The Prince's claws dig into bronze hips when the angel clenches down on him, fluid smearing over his thighs. Pressure builds in the Prince's back as his wings threaten to burst, right up until the last drop leaves him. The Prince hunches forward with a shudder, catching himself on his half-shifted hands, and he finally unseats himself.

He slips out of the angel, gratefully spent, and stares down at his prize. His flightless rosefinch pants heavily beneath him, well and exhausted, not daring to move a finger. A handsome bird indeed, with surprisingly proud features and a body no doubt intended for much more taxing labor than receiving a Prince's pleasure, but here in the underworld, even the most fearsome avenging angel could not escape the diminishing gaze of a self-respecting demon. Pooled in his own freshly fluffed hair, the little rosefinch quietly drifts into unconsciousness. The Prince watches fondly as the angel's seam slowly starts to close again, the bloom shut for the night.

Leaning down, the Night Prince presses a kiss to those flushed lips of skin, and lays down to get some blissful rest. It's not nearly enough to feed him, but they have all the time in the underworld now.

"My Prince."

The Night Prince sighs from his place in bed.

"My Prince, I'm sorry to wake you, but...are you really home?"

With a yawn, the Night Prince waves his hand. "Could this not wait?"

"I'm so sorry, it's just—my Prince, it's been years. No one has heard from you in ages and suddenly, we receive word from the Great Bridge that you have taken a vow with one of the fallen?"

The Night Prince finally pushes himself up, first to glare at the nervous, dog-eared attendant kneeling at his bed, and then to check on the angel. His back is turned to the Prince, pretending rather poorly to be asleep.

"Vows can't be refused if we have no prior arrangements," the Prince states dully. He places a finger on one of the angel's scars, drawing softly over the ruddy gouge just to watch bronze skin cover in goosebumps.

"My Prince, I am so sorry for intruding, but the King requests—ah, he demands you come and see him."

"Of course he does," the Night Prince sighs back. "Last I remember, he doesn't prefer it when I show up smelling like sex, so you'll have to give me a moment."

The angel stiffens at a kiss pressed to his shoulder, and a flick of tongue over his neck, before the Night Prince slides out of bed.

"O-oh, forgive me for intruding."

The attendant scurries away with tail tucked as the Prince makes no attempt to hide himself, softly padding through his quarters to the bath again. He didn't intend on this much mess, but a drought as long as his is bound to have lasting effects. Wading back into the warm water, he sighs his last breath of content before washing up and dressing himself in heavy uniform to go to his father's Court.

The entire journey from the halls of the Night Palace to the Undying Throne, the Prince is followed by a swarm of locusts in the form of whispers.

"Is that the Night Prince?"

"The Pale Prince has returned?"

"Is it really him?"

Chin held high, the Night Prince doesn't spare a glance as the hushed voices build and swell around him.

"The eldest Prince is back from the human world."

The sound of his own name blends into something else as it is repeated over and over again through the halls of the Undying Court. By the time he's in front of his father—neatly dressed in black, not a hair out of place—the entire Undying Court must know he has returned.

His father, the Undying King, straightens up as the Night Prince drifts down the aisle toward him. If the Night Prince was whittled from a moon beam, his father is an eclipse crushed into the shape of a man. His streams of dark hair would not be so different from the angel's, if not for the pallor of death that suffuses every inch of his body, turning his skin ashen and his hair limp. Banishing his nervous attendant with a twitch of his sallow fingers, the Undying King clears the room for the Night Prince to approach the foot of his father's throne.

"Where the fuck have you been?" His father stares from his seat of bone, unimpressed.

"I hit a bit of a snag in the human world," the Prince tells him. "They've gotten very clever up there, you know?"

"You took a vow," his father states, voice swinging low.

The Prince drops his gaze with a smile. "Not even I can say no to those."

"If you had just taken a fucking wife, this wouldn't have happened!"

The Prince's gaze flicks up and back as the Undying King huffs like a bull.

"This is all because you wouldn't make a decision. You ran away to the human world and waited so long that some useless angel took the choice from you."

The Prince does not deny him, and the King rubs at his temples. "Why do you test me like this? I've had to give the Night Court over to your useless cousins, and they've made a mess of everything in your absence. Take control of your damn Court and clean this up."

The Prince nods. "Of course, my King."

"You infuriate me," the King says, quieter. "More and more every year."

The Prince offers a mournful smile. "That pesky blood of mine."

Rolling his eyes, the King slumps over to lean his chin on his fist.

"Speaking of, when is mother due back?" the Prince asks, all innocence.

"Shut your mouth," the King snaps.

"I'm serious, I've been trapped up there for a while, you know?" The Prince relaxes his formal stance to put a hand on his hip. "I lost track of the seasons. When does winter start?"

The King gives a petulant grunt. "A month."

"No wonder you're so happy to see me," the Prince mutters.

"We'll hold a feast for your return." The King gives a snap of his fingers, and another attendant rushes over to him from the edges of the room. "You will attend your own dinner, and you'll bring the damned angel with you to announce your vow. Who is it anyway?"

The Prince gives an elegant shrug. "I asked. He wouldn't answer."

"What did it do?" the King demands.

"He's quite quiet, this one," the Prince says. "You should be impressed."

"You already fucked it, didn't you?"

The Prince resumes his formal posture, folding his hands behind his back.

The King seethes in his direction, white knuckling the edge of his throne. "If you don't keep it under control, I will eat it in front of you. Leave. Miserable boy."

"Glad to be back," the Prince says, offering another low bow before he turns away.

"Go to the Pleasure Garden! At least fuck a demon while you're here. A vow doesn't have to bind your cock too."

The Night Prince doesn't stop walking. "I'll take that under advisement!"

Just past the massive double doors leading into the throne room, the Prince is engulfed in the smell of iron.

"How kind of you to grace us with your presence."

The Night Prince smiles, turning toward the hulking demon posted against the wall with a long pike in hand. The Blood Prince is statuesque as always, almost all of his warm, dark brown skin on display under the scant straps of his dress armor. He would tower over the Night Prince even without his curved bull's horns—if he bothered to get any closer.

"Ward! Did you miss me, little brother?" the Night Prince asks.

"No," Ward says flatly. "You've been here five minutes and already father is pissed off. Your impertinence knows no bounds."

The Night Prince grins. "I love when you compliment me. Come to my feast, won't you?"

"Absolutely not," Ward says, pushing off from the wall. "I want no part of your hedonism. I only came to confirm that you'll be resuming your duties at the Night Court. The place has been in shambles since you threw your tantrum and ran off."

"Don't you worry about a thing," the Night Prince assures him. "I'll fix everything up all nice and neat for you. Were the nights long and cold without me?"

"Hardly," Ward mutters, dipping his hairless head. "Be honest with me, brother. Who had you trapped on the surface?"

The Night Prince touches his chin in thought, then gives a blank look. "It's all such a blur."

Ward glowers at him, brown eyes narrowed. "Fine, don't tell me. I'll leave you to your Pleasure Gardens."

"Oh, I'm not going there." The Night Prince shakes his head. "Believe it or not, that little bird of mine really took it out of me. I'm exhausted."

Ward lets out the softest of displeased groans, but the Night Prince silently appears beside him just to throw his pale arm around Ward's dark shoulder.

"Honestly, I can't remember the last time I had it so good. Wound up rooted in him all night. Poor thing's probably still sleeping off the ache in his cunt. He was a virgin. Isn't that wonderful?"

Ward shakes his shoulder to free himself, but the Night Prince has already danced away. "If you ever want me to set you up, little brother, just say the word," he calls before disappearing from the hall without a trace.

The rosefinch with no wings finds himself alone in a demon Prince's bed, covered in dried fluids, and aching from head to toe.

"I'm alive."

He says it aloud, then covers his mouth as if to keep some secret to himself. He springs up out of bed, only to stop cold when he realizes he has no clothes to wear. Self-consciousness grips him by the scruff, and he tears one of the sheets from the Night Prince's bed to fashion around his body, covering his waist and his scars.

The second time he stops is because he has no idea where anything is. He inches through the Night Prince's living quarters like a mouse scurrying from wall to wall for safety. He creeps past a dining room, a library, and a strange darkened cavern that fills him with dread. This great palace appears to be empty of people, though it is full of beautiful things. Paintings, statues, and human artifacts are lovingly displayed across the spacious, empty halls.

The rosefinch finds himself walking down the largest corridor yet, eyes fixed wide open as he walks by massive murals on the wall that span across the ceiling in an arch above him. Everything looks human-made, perfectly preserved in the Night Prince's home. Before he knows it, the flightless bird is standing on the threshold of the entire palace. He can see the night sky beyond, and fields of grass held in dim starlight. These stars are much too close to be the real night sky of course, but an eternally peaceful version of it.

One cautious step at a time, the rosefinch descends a short staircase, tensed in anticipation of a hand around his throat at any moment. When nothing grabs him and hauls him back inside—his bare feet easing onto soft grass—he perks up again. For some reason, the Night Palace is unguarded, so the rosefinch picks up his pace before anyone notices.

Ahead of him, the soft grasslands slowly descend into a barren stone path leading toward a massive palace lit in bloody red. Even just looking at it is like standing in front of a furnace. Mild heat fills the rosefinch's cheeks and he turns to the left, where the grass thrives and a path of pale flowers invites him down with the light scent of pollen. Moonflowers, datura, lilies, and cereus blooms draw the rosefinch toward a rich and beautiful garden bursting with life.

The closer he gets, the more he can hear voices—laughter and singing, mixed in with music. There are massive tents set up, each one casting a different colored glow onto the people underneath. A warm orange light shows people twirling around a dance floor, a cool blue light bathes people seated on blankets with food all around them. One of the tents appears to be casting an ever-shifting starscape, and when the rosefinch tries to see the bodies underneath, he discerns someone leaning forward on their hands, but as soon as he clocks the telltale thrust of their hips, he tears his gaze away.

There are others on the path with him now, and his shoulders tense as he looks for a way out. He does not wish to get swept up into those tents, so when the walkway splits in two, he hurriedly goes in the direction away from the flowers and the tangle of bodies, toward a circular stone building with much louder shouts and cheers emanating from within. There are demons stationed around the entrance, directing people in two streams.

As the rosefinch is pulled along the river of bodies, a demon asks him, "Ticket?"

"N-no, sorry."

"Standing room only," the demon says, drawing a black line of ink onto the back of his hand.

The crowd thins within the oven-warm building, half of them going up sets of stairs, and everyone with black lines spilling to the level below. The rosefinch swallows a spark of panic, glancing around the horde of demons pushing him further into the building. They are filling into the space beneath the proper seats, threading around columns of stone until the rosefinch gets pressed right up against the waist-high wall above a sandy arena.

He can't quite tell what's going on, but he can feel the bodies squishing into him on all sides as everyone crushes toward the arena to get closer. Bunching his hands in the front of his makeshift skirt, the rosefinch tries to fold himself smaller. The lights go dim around them and the demon to his right gives a low rumbling sound. Someone announces the names of the competitors from the stands above them in a booming voice that bounces off the stone walls. Two svelte demons step onto the sand beneath them, swords in hand, and the crowd presses in even closer to catch a glimpse.

"Second bout!" the announcer calls from above. "At the ready!"

The combatants approach each other, raising their swords level until the tips are aimed at each other. They're not wearing armor, only a few thick leather straps tightly wound around their waists and a scant sheer cloth to cover their hips. One of them has a reptilian tail hanging between their legs, and the other has a steer's horns jutting from their head.

The demon closest to the rosefinch turns his head toward the finch's curtain of dark hair and loudly sniffs as the two swordsmen cautiously approach each other. The rosefinch goes stiff as the demon to his right openly appraises him.

"Set!"

There's a metal clang as the two swords meet in the middle. The combatants slide their weapons lengthwise until only the tips of steel are touching, and the two swords become a straight line of silver linking their wielders. The two demons lock eyes, connected through the very points of their weapons.

"Start!"

Both their bodies tense, and then they dart forward so quickly, the rosefinch can't focus on their limbs, their swords vanishing in the quickness of their slashes.

"You smell nice." A demon breathes in the rosefinch's ear. "Like you want something."

The rosefinch straightens up, body heat pulsing around him from every side as he notices the demon bent down to whisper to him.

"I don't want anything," the rosefinch replies, eyes on the arena but he's too panicked to focus on the fight.

The demon nearly presses his nose to the rosefinch's fluffed hair and inhales deeply. "Where are you from anyway? You smell like Night Court but you don't look like Night Court."

"'Course he's not Night Court," the demon to his left pipes up. "He's *working* for Night Court. Isn't that right? You're from the Gardens?"

The two demons are facing him, each of the rosefinch's shoulders pressed to their chests.

"No…" the rosefinch mutters.

"He smells like the Prince," the bulkier one says to his companion, brushing some of the finch's dark hair aside.

"Prince has been gone for years," his friend says. "But I see what you mean." He sticks his nose in close and the rosefinch tries to turn away, to no avail. "Aw, he's shy. Must be new."

The one on his left smiles through his words, each syllable shaving away on the points of his fangs.

"We'll pay nice if you keep quiet." The one on his right puts a heavy hand on the rosefinch's shoulder, sliding thick fingers across his collarbone.

"Might pay nicer if you make a fuss though." The one on his left pulls on the front of the rosefinch's makeshift skirt. His fingers look coated in a layer of char but it doesn't leave a mark as he presses hard on the finch's body, searching through the fabric for something to touch.

The rosefinch jerks away, only for the larger demon to catch his arm and hold him there.

"Huh?" The skinny one cups his hand between the finch's thighs with a look of surprise. "He doesn't have anything."

"What do you mean 'he doesn't have anything'?" The big one grabs the finch's shoulders and forcibly turns him to face his companion. "Look harder."

The skinny demon yanks up the edges of rosefinch's silk sheet, and his eyes pop open wide as he smirks.

"Shit, I think this is one of those fallen—"

A pale hand extends out through the darkness behind them to clamp tight around the demon's mouth.

"He doesn't work for the Night Court. He *belongs* to the Night Court."

The wiry demon lets go of the rosefinch's skirt, and the larger one snaps his hand back like he's been burned.

"W-we didn't know, Prince," the wiry one sputters, backing against the wall. "He's not wearing your colors! And he didn't say anything!"

The Night Prince swoops in, his chest to the rosefinch's back, and grabs both the demon's by their scruffs, bending their bodies over the chest-high wall.

"He doesn't need my colors when he wears my scent. You should know better."

The Prince leans down to nuzzle his face to the top of the rosefinch's hair. "You gave me a scare when you weren't where I left you. What did these terrible demons do to you? Be honest."

Swallowing his own frantic pulse, the rosefinch looks between the two demons held in supplication, the whites of their eyes showing as they stare at the arena below.

"W-we didn't mean anything, really!" the wiry demon pleads.

"They..." The rosefinch swallows, throat burning. "They thought I was someone else. I should have spoken up faster."

The Night Prince sighs against his rosefinch's hair, and the crisp scent of pine fills the air.

"My bird is new here," the Prince says to the demons. "So he doesn't know the rules. That when you are in my Court, you are not to touch my things. And if you break that rule, well..."

The crowd suddenly erupts into cheering as the combatants below finish their duel, one bloody sword held up high, the other laying beside its prone owner.

"I can see I've been away for far too long," the Night Prince says with a sigh.

A rush of harsh wind bursts through the room, and the Prince tosses the two demons over the wall and into the arena. The rosefinch doesn't get to see them land as the Prince pulls the finch's hips against his body and whisks them both up onto the second level of seating in the blink of an eye. The rosefinch clings to the Prince just to keep his legs under him as he glances around the rows of finely dressed demons. It's a bit brighter on the second level, pyres burning near the open roof which show the stars high above. The finch is sorely out of place in his rumpled sheet. Even the Night Prince dons a finely fit uniform of black and silver.

"I have your next combatants," the Night Prince announces, and though he doesn't raise his voice, it's in everyone's ears all the same. "I found these two thieves lurking below. The loser will be punished for both of them."

Every single demon in the room straightens their spines. The Night Prince sweeps the rosefinch down the aisle and into an empty pair of seats set apart from the rest of the well-dressed demons. Of course, he doesn't allow the rosefinch to actually take the empty seat, but pulls him into the Prince's lap instead.

"Every High Court has their sport of choice," the Prince explains to his bird. "This is ours."

The rosefinch shivers as the announcer's voice rings through the crowd once more—announcing in a stunned voice that the Night Prince himself has come to witness their next match. The Night Prince's large arms wind around the finch's waist.

"Are they going to kill each other?" the rosefinch asks in a hush.

The Prince laughs low in his ear, trailing his hand over the rosefinch's thigh. "You can't kill a demon in the underworld, not really. But pain is very real."

The rosefinch squirms at the Prince's touch, long pale fingers plucking at the sheet. It's difficult to tell in the dim light, but the spectators all seem torn between the new pair of demons getting stripped down for a fight, and the return of the Night Prince now casually joined by a companion in his long-vacant arena seat.

"You haven't bathed," the Night Prince whispers. "I'm surprised. I always thought angels prized cleanliness. Or do you just like wearing my mess?"

He turns the rosefinch's face toward his with a wolfish smile. "It's no wonder those demons put their hands on you. You smell like cum."

The rosefinch shrinks in on himself, and the Night Prince brushes his nose against the finch's cheek.

"I don't mind, of course, but you should know that's an open invitation to a demon in the Gardens out here. I would have gladly given you this advice if you'd *stayed where I left you.*"

The demons in the arena have been given swords and tension sinks into their limbs as they face each other for the chance to escape punishment.

"I...got lost," the rosefinch admits.

"You're the one who demanded a vow, didn't you?" the Night Prince murmurs into the rosefinch's cheek, his hand pulling up the edge of the sheet. "I can't very well protect you if you go wandering off, now can I? You're not even dressed in Court clothing."

The two demons below touch the points of their swords together as the announcer narrates.

The rosefinch's breathing shortens up. He barely gets the words out to say, "I'm sorry."

The Prince softly sighs as he slips his hand under the makeshift skirt to run his thumb over the rosefinch's seam.

"I almost believe you," the Prince says through his smile as the rosefinch's skin rouses once more. "Did you open when they touched you?"

He asks as he traces the slowly softening lips of skin, and the rosefinch shakes his head over and over, *no.*

"You know, we could be partners if you were honest with me," the Prince coos. "Tell me what got you sent down here, and I'll put an end to this show."

The two demons in the arena are staring at each other as enemies, and everyone in the stands has leaned down to watch with interest.

"Every single being in this room answers to me," the Prince says, and the rosefinch twitches as his body goes slick where those pale fingers touch him. It's happening so much faster this time. "Except you, apparently."

The rosefinch fights the desire to go weak with the Prince's fingers slipping inside his body. That seam has barely opened but he's dripping wet at the pressure. His hands snap to the armrests while the Prince slides his fingers around the buried head of his cock. He doesn't remember all this messy fluid, but most of the previous night is a blur to him now.

"Fine, don't talk." The Night Prince doesn't sound all that disappointed as he swirls his thumb over the slit in the rosefinch's cock. "Who's winning the bout?"

The rosefinch jerks his hips back into the Prince's, like he means to get free of the Prince's hands, but there's nowhere to go when he's already in the demon's arms. He can't stop his cock from hardening up in the Prince's hand, slowly slipping out past his seam and sticking to the front of the sheet.

"Tell me what's happening in the duel or I'll make you shout in front of all these people," the Prince threatens in a whisper with a squeeze of the finch's stem.

The rosefinch hunches forward, sweat gathering along his back as his thighs tense. He wants to close his eyes, he wants to run away, he wants to spread his legs and get this searing heat out of him as fast as possible, but he forces himself to focus on the arena. The two demons are both bleeding from their arms as they once again touch the points of their swords against each other's.

"T-they're both hurt," the rosefinch pants. "I c-can't tell who's winning."

"It's a subtle sport," the Prince murmurs, fingers gliding over the rosefinch's slick cock. "The duelists resume their opening stance after any blood has been drawn. You only have two minutes to render your opponent useless, or else you both lose. If you touch the wall, you lose. If your sword breaks, or you drop your weapon, you lose. You can touch each other with your hands, but the moment you spill blood, you have to reset."

The skinny demon's feet are sliding backward on the sandy floor as his companion physically forces him toward the wall, two huge hands clamped around his shoulders. The rosefinch's eyes are trying to close as the Prince leisurely plays with his cock.

"You're so wet," the Prince notes, gaze on the stain spreading over the front of the sheet—now tented from the tip of the finch's erection. "Who do you think will win?"

"The stronger one," the rosefinch chokes out, goosebumps shooting down his chest and arms as he throbs against the Prince's palm. "He's b-backing the small one into the wall."

The larger demon is nearly twice the size of his companion and having no trouble at all strong-arming his friend across the floor. The rosefinch is putting all of his effort into keeping his voice under control while the Prince traces the shape of him like he has all the time in the world.

"You don't have as much skin as a demon..." The Prince speaks into the rosefinch's shoulder as he massages yet more drops of fluid from the finch's slit. "Smaller too. Almost like a human."

Embarrassment floods the rosefinch's face, but he can feel the Prince getting aroused underneath him. A thick line of heat presses into the curve of his ass, and he almost misses as the skinny demon below suddenly darts forward, slashing wildly as his counterpart goes hurtling into the stone wall without anything to stop his momentum.

The crowd cheers its approval, and the skinny demon drops his weapon out of sheer relief.

The Prince presses a kiss to the rosefinch's shoulder. "Shall I get you out of here before everyone notices what a mess you are?"

"*Yes,*" the rosefinch hisses.

Adjusting his arms, the Prince hoists the rosefinch up, gives a stately wave to the arena of spectators, and leaves. The room turns to a smear of paint, and by the time the Prince has fully straightened his legs, they are back in the washroom of the Night Palace. The rosefinch lets his breath out as he sees they are alone, and the Prince sets his bare feet down in the shallowest part of the bath.

"Take this filthy thing off," the Prince says with a smile, tugging at the bed sheet. "I never would have expected an angel to cloak themself in such a mess. You are full of surprises."

The rosefinch's shoulders go tense, but he doesn't fight the Prince undressing him.

"Around the Palace is one thing, but if you have to go wandering off, then you need to dress accordingly." Slipping his hands around the rosefinch's face, the Night Prince forces their gazes back together. "You belong to me. Every demon should know just by looking at you that you're mine. Maybe then they won't be so cavalier with your body."

The rosefinch stares into full-moon eyes. "I suppose...that right is reserved for you?"

"Now you're getting it," the Prince says with a handsome smile. "There's only one man who outranks me in the underworld. And he never comes to my Court. I am a king here."

Dragging his hands down over the rosefinch's chest, the Prince lightly plucks on the finch's nipple, drawing out a gasp.

"You are a lovely mess, but I shouldn't bring you to the tailor like this," the Prince says. He pulls his hands back to start unbuttoning his own black jacket. This uniform is not entirely unfamiliar to the rosefinch, a regal ensemble that unnecessarily accentuates the body underneath. All demons above a certain station wear some version of it, but those demons don't share the Night Prince's certain *earthly* beauty.

Weak in the legs, the rosefinch sinks down to kneel in the running water, but the warmth pouring over his hips and thighs isn't doing anything to lessen the adrenaline. He snaps his gaze away from the sight of his own unfamiliar body—those can't possibly be his hips, split open and throbbing. Scooting back on the sloped floor, the rosefinch puts his head under the water spout, staunchly ignoring the Pale Prince as he strips down once again and joins the rosefinch in the water.

"Two baths in one day." The Prince lays down in the shallow pool, propping his head up on his fist and running his other hand along the rosefinch's leg. "I'm really playing the part of a royal."

The rosefinch startles at the Prince's cool touch in the warm water while his skin burns with pleasure he doesn't want.

"What will you do with those demons?" the rosefinch asks.

"Tell me why you went wandering off, and I'll tell you their fate," the Prince says, leaning down to kiss a bronze knee.

The rosefinch only watches the way his pale pink lips press against the curve of flesh.

"They said..." The rosefinch swallows as the Prince licks his thigh. "They said you'd been gone for years."

"Mm." The Prince inches closer, picking up the finch's leg so he can slither between flushed thighs. "Technically I wasn't supposed to be gone for so long, but the human world is a dangerous place, even for someone as powerful as me. And humans are very desperate creatures. But that's a boring story. I need to get you cleaned up. You're expected."

The rosefinch stares at the Prince's smiling face, slowly pulling his legs away from that lecherous gaze.

"I can do it," the rosefinch says.

"You've had such a long day," the Prince coos. "Lie down. I'll do it."

The rosefinch opens his mouth, only to shut it a moment later. Face hot, he slowly lays on his back, letting the water chase down the sides of his body, spilling over his arms and legs.

"That's a good little bird," the Prince says, pushing water up onto the rosefinch's stomach. He slides his hands down the finch's torso, and the rosefinch's mouth pinches as his nipples go hard under the Prince's palms. When the Prince licks the tip of the rosefinch's cock, he startles forward.

"Not there!"

The Night Prince tilts his head, nudging with his thumb and watching the finch's cock twitch. "You don't want the tailor to see you like this, do you? When I can so easily fix it."

He doesn't wait for an answer, just swallows the rosefinch in a breath, and the finch slaps a hand into the inch of running water. His hips press up without permission, and the Prince slips his arms under the finch's thighs, dropping his face down until his lips are pressed against hairless bronze skin. The rosefinch's strangled moan echoes through the washroom until it blends into the sound of running water. The Night Prince's tongue is a terrible thing that winds around the finch's cock like a fist, but the pleasure is even worse.

The rosefinch has no fight left to give, falling limp as the Prince leeches the poison from him once more in shuddering pulses. His vision starts to blacken at the edges, lovely numbness spreading through his legs. There are no words in his head, just mindless mumbling as he squirms around in the water like a cub trying to escape his mother's tongue.

The Prince doesn't stop sucking until the rosefinch is on the verge of losing consciousness, pulling his mouth off just to lick any excess up for himself.

"You carry a lot of poison for such a little bird."

The rosefinch tries and fails to raise his hand up, dropping it back to the water with a soft splash.

The Prince laughs low. "Don't worry. I'll feed you soon."

The rosefinch is hardly conscious as the Prince finishes washing him. His temples tingle with a strange sensation, and he can barely move his body from some unknown weight. By the time the Prince has brought him back to bed, he is floating in a dark, numb ocean.

"Open your mouth," the Prince says from very far away.

The rosefinch tries, eyelids much too heavy as something presses against his lips. The Prince is attempting to kiss him—or, no, he is passing a slice of sweet fruit from his tongue to his bird's. Bite by bite, the Prince feeds his rosefinch by the mouth until the bird can open his eyes again.

"You're mortal when you're down here," the Prince cautious. "Don't forget to eat. Would be a shame to lose you before we've really had our fun."

The rosefinch lets the Prince cradle his head and raise a cup for him to drink from.

"There is no sunlight in the Night Court. You'll have to get your energy elsewhere."

The rosefinch reaches for the plate held in the Prince's hand, and the Prince smiles before pulling the plate up higher just so he can keep feeding his bird himself.

"Sleep for a little while," the Prince says when the rosefinch's mouth is full again. "And don't go running off, or I'll have to do something rash."

He swans out of sight, and the rosefinch willingly crashes back to sleep. It's hard to dream in this place, and when the Prince wakes him up again, it feels as though no time at all has passed. At least his body is no longer numb.

"I got you a robe," the Prince says, folding it onto a small table beside the bed. "The tailor is looking forward to seeing you, but I need to be clear about how this works."

The Prince leans onto the bed, his hands bracketing the rosefinch's head on the sheets. His handsome face really is almost human, save for the peculiar look of his skin—moonlight on dark water—and the hunger of his teeth.

"I may be the Night Prince, but my absence has not gone unnoticed. I can't have my authority come into question right now, which means I need you to be on my side. I don't know why you came here, or why you were so insistent on that ritual, but you got it. If you do well today, I'll give you something in return. Deal?"

The demon speaks sharp words coated in honey.

"...What will you give me?" the rosefinch asks so quietly.

The Prince smiles too wide, revealing his teeth with pleasure. "I'm the eldest son of the Undying King. What can't I give you?"

The rosefinch holds his gaze, bathed in the strange glow of the Pale Prince, and nods his head.

"Come and eat a little more," the Prince beckons. "Can't have you passing out at the tailor. They'll think I'm mistreating you."

He slips his hand around the rosefinch's and pulls him gently from the bed to drape the robe around his shoulders. There is an embarrassment of food waiting in the Night Prince's personal dining room. He seats himself at the head of the table, but not before pulling out a chair for the rosefinch. And there the bird sits while the eldest Prince of Hell watches him eat.

"Th…" The rosefinch swallows to wet his throat. "Thank you for not killing me."

The Prince gives him an amused smirk. "I can't. As per the rules of the ritual."

"B-but you said—" the rosefinch sputters, only to cut himself short when the Prince gives a quiet laugh.

"Don't you know, little bird? Demons love to lie."

The rosefinch finishes eating in pouting silence, and the Night Prince basks in it.

When it's time for their appointment, the Prince takes the rosefinch's waist once more and whisks them both away in a silent rush of wind and smoke. They settle in a cavernous hall, cast in a warm, gold glow. If the Night Palace is meant to evoke a calm summer night, this place is the inside of an overstuffed treasure chest.

"With me," the Prince says, pulling the rosefinch along. He tightens his grip on the rosefinch's waist. "I can't have you getting stolen away from me."

"Is this where the tailor lives?" the rosefinch asks, eyes drawn to paintings in gilded frames, and jewelry on pedestals.

"Yes. This is my sister's Court, so we'll have to ask her permission. And so long as we're in the Hungry Palace, I won't let you out of my sight. Things have a tendency to go missing here."

They walk past increasingly large arrangements of treasure until the walls are barely visible behind the shine of gold. The rosefinch almost doesn't see the two winged guards in splendid, jeweled armor adorning their black feathers, each standing on either side of an open archway. One of them steps into the room beyond to announce them, extending their long neck to caw.

"The Pale Prince of Night and his bond!"

The Night Prince sweeps the rosefinch into a cozy throne room, similarly lined with trinkets and treasures and sculptures. Atop her throne of gold, the Hungry Prince sits with her thick legs dangling over one armrest, and her head hanging over the other, a curtain of light brown hair unspooled around thick goat's horns. Three demons are splayed out on the rug beneath her chair, twined together like a living chain. The rosefinch tries not to look at the bacchanal display—one plump demon strung between two others with their mouth too full to speak.

"Brother!" The Hungry Prince claps her hands together. "Oh, Ward tried to tell me you died."

The Night Prince smiles serenely. "I'm sure he prayed every night for my bloody demise. How are you, sweet sister?"

"Much better now that you're home," she says.

The Hungry Prince rises from her throne with the audible jangling of metal draped over her body. Strands of beautiful gold jewelry loosely hug every generous curve, rippling over warm, gold skin as she gestures to the threesome unraveling at her feet.

"Everyone's been very touchy, but when I realized you were back, it all made sense. I hope you don't mind," she says.

The Night Prince steps forward and offers his hand, holding it just above the head of the demon on their knees, quietly fucking the one held in the middle. They're barely restraining their groaning as the *plap, plap, plap* of skin on skin grows louder. The Hungry Prince takes her brother's hand and presses his knuckles to her forehead, right between her two spired goat's horns.

"I missed you!" she says.

The Night Prince smooths his thumb over her face. "I missed you too."

The rosefinch flinches as one of the demons on the floor grabs the hem of his robe, drawing his gaze to the one in the middle as their legs go taut like a bowstring, their own hand haphazardly pawing at their clit.

"Does he play?" the Hungry Prince asks, leveling her black gaze on the rosefinch. She wraps her arms around the closest demon on their knees, pushing her hands through their hair as their face pinches in pleasure. "We love making friends, and we never get angels."

She slides her finger into the demon's panting mouth, hushing their rattling moans.

The Night Prince's fingers tighten on the rosefinch's hip. "Now that does sound fun."

Heat skitters down the rosefinch's spine like burning pebbles. The demon in the middle lets go of the rosefinch's robe in favor of the demon with her cock down their throat. They pull on her hips as fluid wells up around their lips.

"You were away for so long, and now that you're back, you've gone and wound everyone up," the Hungry Prince has an innocent face, though her smile is anything but. "I can tell you need it too. I'm honestly shocked you're out so soon. You must be freezing. Stay a while. Warm up with us."

The demon hunched over the face of her companion snaps her tail against the stone floor with a grunt, cradling the demon's head between her thighs.

With a deep breath, the Night Prince surveys the scene with longing. "Unfortunately, father expects us for a feast later. I came here to ask if we could borrow your tailor."

The Hungry Prince pouts. "Not even a little?"

The Night Prince shuffles the rosefinch in front of him, opening the silky robe so the Hungry Prince can see the closed lips of skin.

"Hairless. How cute," she says. "I'd love to see how he moves."

"He only opens for me," the Prince explains, hands on the rosefinch's thighs. "It would take more time than we have."

The Hungry Prince narrows her eyes, head tilting slightly. "My dear brother, are you sure you're quite well? If Ward catches you weakened, he won't hesitate. Even at your own feast."

The Night Prince looks fondly at the tightening threesome as the demons writhe against each other, desperately trying not to interrupt the royalty as they chase their fever-induced bliss.

"Maybe just a little," the Prince says.

The Hungry Prince claps her hands and twirls around the pile of demons. "Let's see the tailor. Their assistants can help us out."

"M-my Prince?" one of the demons chokes out, whining from their place on the floor.

"You three stay here," the Hungry Prince says. "I'll be back soon enough."

The Hungry Prince leads the way through her palace of bronze and gold, past a cavernous banquet hall, and even more stockpiles of numbingly beautiful treasure. The air smells of rich food and potent wine. The Hungry Prince is not imposing in height, but she looks at everything with a sharp eye, and the rosefinch finds himself drifting closer to the Night Prince.

And of course, the Night Prince responds with his arm twined around the rosefinch's shoulders, his hand resting on the finch's bare chest.

"He'll need entirely new clothes, right?" The Hungry Prince steals another glance at the rosefinch, and he shies away. It's like she's tasting him with every flick of her gaze.

"They don't exactly send angels down here with suitcases," the Night Prince responds. "All he has is this robe."

"Well he'll be in good hands with Oma." The Hungry Prince gives a sweet laugh as she guides them into a workshop lined with bolts of fabric in every conceivable color and pattern. "But you'll owe me a favor, brother."

"Of course, sweet sister."

She laughs as she pours herself onto a long couch and whistles. "Oma! You have a job."

From behind a rack of fabric, a spindly demon slinks into the room. There are three sets of arms hinged down their back, and their shoulders appear to be capped in a bright yellow chitin.

"Mistress," the spidery demon, Oma, bows to the Hungry Prince.

"You remember my brother?" The Hungry Prince gestures behind her toward the Night Prince, and Oma turns to drop into a slightly more formal bow with their arm swept under their chest.

"My Prince," Oma says.

The Night Prince smiles. "I trust you're enjoying your work since I loaned you to the Hungry Palace?"

"Yes, my Prince," Oma says, rising back up and turning their shiny black eyes onto the rosefinch.

"Is this our client?"

The Night Prince withdraws his hands so he can gently push the rosefinch toward Oma.

"I'm expected to introduce him at a feast in my honor. He needs to wear the Night's colors, and he needs..." The Night Prince slips his hands over the rosefinch's shoulders to pull the edges of the robe away. "To show his scars."

The rosefinch twitches as his gouges are laid bare in front of yet more people. The hours have already softened some of the scarlet into a ruddy, bruised color, but there's no mistaking what they are.

"He needs to leave with clothes for the feast, but he needs a full wardrobe as well. You can send those to the Night Palace as you finish them."

"Well then, we won't waste any time," Oma says, guiding the rosefinch to stand on a low stone platform, only a few inches high.

More spidery demons emerge from behind the racks of fabric, quietly slinking in to take the rosefinch's measurements. The Night Prince backs away to sit on the couch opposite his sister, and someone removes the finch's silk robe entirely—with a much gentler presence. The demons are nearly silent as they hold up the rosefinch's arms and pull strands of silk across his skin to measure him. The rosefinch stiffens as they cinch more silk around his bare hips.

"My brother has been too busy to properly eat since he came home," the Hungry Prince announces. "He's feeling a little tired. Let's give him something nice to look at while we wait for the clothes."

"Of course, mistress," Oma says. They hold a sketchbook and pencil in two hands, but two of their other palms open in invitation. "Raph."

One of the demons pauses in the middle of measuring the rosefinch's feet. At once, a pair of gentle hands snaps tight around the finch's ankle, another pair cupping the finch's thigh. The demon looks up at the rosefinch with eight small eyes dotted over his face.

The rosefinch immediately looks at the Night Prince, but the heavily lidded gaze of the eldest demon Prince is as good as useless to him. Raph leans his face against the rosefinch's thigh, inching up onto the stone pedestal with him, and the rosefinch burns as the rest of the demons finish taking his measurements and drift over to pick fabrics and begin work.

Two hands smooth over the rosefinch's hips, and Raph gently touches the closed lips of skin with his thumb.

"Does it open?" Raph asks, nudging at the folds.

The rosefinch raises his chin, red in the face as goosebumps shoot down his legs. "No."

"Hm." Raph tilts his head and decides to turn the rosefinch around, all six of his hands spinning the rosefinch toward the couch where the Night Prince now lounges.

The rosefinch meets the Night Prince's pale gaze with an indignant curl to his lip—until the spider demon nestles his face against the rosefinch's skin, his breath warm on the finch's backside.

The rosefinch's shoulders stiffen, and the Night Prince's smile widens.

"What is it?" the Night Prince asks.

Raph holds the rosefinch in place as his tongue snakes out to lick untouched skin. The rosefinch cranes around to look back in horror at the demon spreading him open with two hands.

"No!" the rosefinch gives a manic chirp, attempting to swat him away, but Raph only catches both the finch's wrists, and his thighs, immobilizing the bird where he stands with all those extra limbs.

"Why not there?"

The rosefinch turns back toward the Night Prince only to find him standing a few inches away, eyes alight with burning interest.

The rosefinch's legs twitch as he feels the demon's tongue laving at his hole. "It's not r-right."

Raph is slowly pushing the rosefinch's legs apart.

"Why do you think you were made like this?" the Night Prince asks. With the inches of the stone pedestal, the rosefinch is even closer to the demon's full-moon eyes.

"Like what?" the rosefinch demands in a wavering voice as Raph's tongue presses harder, trying to slip inside him.

The Night Prince smiles so softly, cupping the finch's face in his hands. "Your body loves to be touched."

"No," the rosefinch squeaks out with the tip of Raph's tongue wetting his insides.

"Your precious gods gave you countless ways to experience pleasure, and then locked them all away to keep you obedient. Now that you're free of their gaze, shouldn't you get to enjoy it?"

The rosefinch shakes his head, unable to move with Raph holding his arms, and the Night Prince muttering obscenities. His pale hands bring heat as he draws his fingers down the finch's neck.

"You blush so easily, little rosefinch," the Night Prince whispers. "Even more than a human."

In the wake of the Prince's fingertips, the finch's body weakens. He moans as Raph's tongue quite suddenly spears deeper inside him, and the Night Prince catches the sound with his own mouth.

The finch's eyes fly open with the Night Prince's tongue snaking over his own, and Raph's busy between his thighs. He trembles, and when Raph releases his wrists, the finch only grabs onto the Night Prince's waist to keep himself from collapsing.

When the Night Prince pulls away, he glances down at the finch's hips with a smile.

"Self-conscious, are we?"

The folds of skin are flushed—dark and swollen, the slight shine of welling fluid about to drip free—but still they remain closed.

"How sweet," the Night Prince says, thumbs smoothing over the finch's face. "You only want me to see."

The finch is panting, legs threatening to give in, so the Night Prince kindly slides his hand down the finch's spine to touch the top of Raph's head.

"Thank you for your service."

Raph pulls his face back, taking a deep breath, and bows his head. "Of course, my Prince." His breathing is ragged.

"Is that it?" The Hungry Prince laughs from across the room. "Has a vow dulled you so quickly, brother?"

"I'm afraid I've come down with a rotten possessiveness," the Night Prince calmly explains. "Let the spiders handle it."

The Hungry Prince claps her hands. "Another to play with Raph, please!"

Raph slowly backs away from the stone pedestal, eight eyes slowly going glassy. He sits on the floor, a bit dazed as another of Oma's assistants kneels down to kiss him. Almost immediately, the new demon startles, a shiver chasing up their spine, and then they kiss Raph to the floor with feverish intent.

The Hungry Prince laughs low. "They'll be drunk off your angel for days."

All eight of Raph's limbs squirm uselessly over the ground as his partner wrestles his trousers down his thighs. The rosefinch can't look away that time. Did he do something to them? The spiders' arms lace around each other as their hips stutter together, no grace, only need.

The Night Prince slips his hands around the finch's hips.

"Skirt or trousers for the feast?" Oma asks, ignoring their moaning assistants as they look at the Night Prince.

"Skirt, of course," the Night Prince answers. "We have to dance, after all."

"We do?" The rosefinch turns to him, frowning.

The Night Prince smiles back. "Don't worry. I'll lead."

The rosefinch looks away as two more spider demons approach the pedestal with fabric in hand. The Night Prince lets them take his place, and they begin to fit the rosefinch more precisely into a dress. The finch avoids looking at himself in the three floor length mirrors, but the Night Prince catches his eye in the reflection with a smirk.

Raph lets out a cry from the floor, and the rosefinch startles. "Isn't that distracting?"

Neither of the spider assistants emote.

"Spiders are night creatures," one of them says.

"Whatever feeds the night also feeds us," the other finishes.

The rosefinch flushes as the unrestrained moans of the spiders behind them fill the room. The fitting doesn't take long with so many demons working simultaneously. They get the precise measurements they need, Oma gets approval from the Night Prince on their final design, and they sew him into a beautiful dress in the blink of an eye. The garment is made of several black panels layered around each other with slivers of silver that wink like distant stars when the finch moves. Oma instructs the finch to spin in place, and only mid-motion does the finch realize that his dress opens like the petals of a black rose.

The back of the dress is, of course, fully open and fluttering softly against the finch's skin.

The Hungry Prince rises up to pinch the rosefinch's cheek. "Beautiful! You know, you have lucked yourself into quite an enviable position, little bird," she says to him. "Watch your back. Someone may try to take your place if you're not careful."

She winks at the finch and kisses her brother's hand again. "I'll see you at the feast, my love."

With a cloak draped over the finch's shoulders, the Prince and the finch depart from the tailor to the sound of two spiders drunk off the rosefinch's taste. The finch is surprised when the Night Prince doesn't immediately spirit them back to the Night Palace in a rush of wind, but instead walks them to a small, open-air train station. There are demons coming and going from small hanging train cars, all of them dressed in uniforms delineating the palace they're coming from. None of them are dressed in black like the Night Prince.

"We're taking the scenic route home," the Prince explains to the finch as he flags a station attendant down.

The finch waits until they're seated in an empty train car, drifting slowly over the fields between the Hungry Palace and the Night Palace, to speak again.

"This place is so much different from where I landed..." he mutters, eyes on the endless verdant fields and towering palaces in the distance.

"You landed in a different Court," the Night Prince explains. "We are in the deepest part of the underworld, closest to my father. He prefers things a certain, *old-fashioned* way. But the Courts closer to the surface tend to resemble the human world."

When the finch gets the stomach for it, he turns to face the Night Prince again.

"Are you tired?"

The Night Prince looks at him, the same peaceful smile lifting his handsome mouth, as all of the windows turn pitch black, concealing them from the outside world.

"Why do you ask?"

The rosefinch startles, glancing around the suddenly much smaller train car. "I, uh, meant no disres—"

"I am the Pale Prince of Night, firstborn son of the Undying King, and heir to the throne of the Underworld." The Prince takes the finch's face in his thumb and index finger, pinching firmly. "If you want your position secured here, you will not speak of weakness that doesn't exist."

The rosefinch's eyes widen, heart pounding in his chest as the Prince's gaze seems to swallow him whole.

"You have nothing to fear with me at your side," the demon says.

The rosefinch wordlessly nods.

The Prince tilts his head and all the light comes streaming back as the windows clear up once more.

"Any more questions?" the Prince asks.

The rosefinch swallows, sweat prickling across his neck as he considers his words. "What exactly feeds the night?"

The Prince leans back in his seat, head resting against the wood paneling of the car. "The night is many things. It *allows* for many things. Sometimes it brings fear of the dark, other times it brings permission. The night keeps secrets that the day would spoil."

The rosefinch squirms beside him, playing with the edges of his new cloak. "So, you are fed by the things that happen in the night?"

"Sometimes," the Prince says. "Sometimes it's much simpler than that."

"How..." The rosefinch swallows, trying to wet his throat before he braves another look at the Night Prince. "How do I feed you?"

The Night Prince tilts his head, eyes lidded and hungry. "Everything you do feeds me, my little flightless bird."

The rosefinch's face flushes, and the Night Prince slides his cool fingers under the finch's chin, much gentler this time.

"How mysterious you are. Are you sure you don't want to tell me how you fell?"

The rosefinch holds his gaze, shoulders hunched. "Not any more than you want to tell me why you were gone for so long."

For a second, fear beats through the pulse in the finch's neck as the Prince goes perfectly still, only for the tension to break as he throws his head back and laughs. "Not so shy after all."

Looping his arm around the finch's waist, the Prince sweeps the finch into his lap and dives his hand between the finch's thighs.

"No," the finch grabs his wrist, but the Prince only laughs.

"I thought you wanted to feed me?" he coos.

"The dress..." the finch mutters, face igniting as the Prince slides his fingers between the folds of fabric. "It's new."

The Prince presses his face to the finch's hair and breathes in deep. "Then don't ruin it."

The finch holds his breath as the Prince finds his seam, sliding a long finger down the length of it and holding still as they silently travel through the underworld. He doesn't force, he doesn't even press, just cups the lips of skin, soaking in the finch's embarrassed squirming.

The finch's body wants to open. It wants to suck the Prince in deeper, meet his cool dry skin with the finch's own wet warmth, but the rosefinch grips the front of the Prince's jacket, clenching as tight as he can to keep from spilling fluid onto the pretty new dress. The trip to the Night Palace is several aching minutes longer, and the finch shivers at his own softening body. The Prince's finger has sunk deeper between folds of skin, barely keeping a few drops of slick from spilling down the finch's thighs, when their car finally comes to a stop.

The finch takes a deep breath, body relaxing as the Night Prince withdraws his hand.

"Very good," he says before putting his finger into his mouth to taste. His eyes flash, and he gives a quiet sigh. "It really is like nothing else."

The finch burns, jumping up from the seats to go stand by the door. The matching station in the Night Palace is utterly empty of either attendants or visitors. As the finch looks around the cavernous black stone hall, the Prince strides past him.

"How quickly loyalty burns away when you're not there to stoke the fires," the Night Prince says with a dramatic sigh. "Ah, well. I'll have to find us some more attendants before the feast."

He walks off, and the finch goes after him. "How much time do we have?"

"A few hours at most," the Night Prince says. "I need to do some work, so I'll have to leave you until then."

Catching the finch's hand and bringing it to his mouth, the Prince says, "I trust you will not get into trouble the moment I'm gone?"

The finch shakes his head.

"Stay in my quarters," the Prince instructs. "So no one else tries to eat you."

"I will," the finch answers.

"Good." The Prince smoothly twines their arms together and sets off with the finch in tow, walking them all the way back to his bedroom before he takes his leave with a bow. The finch startles at the gesture, not enough time to think of how to respond before the Prince vanishes.

With a sigh, the finch immediately removes his clothes, hunting around the Prince's personal quarters until he manages to find a long tunic to wriggle into. It is comically large on him, but he just rolls the sleeves up, grateful it covers his hips. Before long, his stomach drives him back to the dining table, still somehow laden with fresh, hot food, which the finch hesitantly pecks at until his stomach finally feels full, and he curls up in the Prince's enormous bed to sleep it off.

He wakes to the sound of people chattering in the room.

"Isn't he dainty?"

"No horns or wings or tail or anything!"

"He's practically human."

The finch bolts upright to see three bat-winged demons surveying him, black eyes shining, muzzles open.

"Hello?" The finch pulls a sheet up over his legs.

The demons laugh at the gesture.

"Oh, look at that. Don't worry, birdie, we're here on orders from the Night Prince," one with black wings says.

"Which means, no touching," another with gold wings adds.

"We're loyal to our Prince, and therefore, loyal to you," the last one with reddish fur says.

All three of them offer sweeping bows with wings neatly tucked, and the rosefinch flinches away.

"Oh. Uh."

The bats straighten up, smirking all three of them.

"We're the Prince's personal attendants," the one with black wings says. "We have clothes for you from the Hungry Palace, and gifts from all over Hell."

"Gifts?" the finch asks, brows furrowed.

The bats all look delighted, muzzles opening in glee.

"For your wedding to the Pale Prince of Night," the one with gold wings explains. "Many have tried and failed before you to win that role. Lucky boy."

"Is that what this feast is for?" the finch sputters, scrambling forward on his hands. "Are we getting married tonight?"

"No, of course not," the ruddy bat waves her hand, offering the finch a glass of water. "Tonight is only an announcement. You'll get real wedding gifts after your vows are made official. Assuming you don't die before then."

The black-winged bat gives the finch a wink. "We won't let that happen. Call me Faye."

"I'm Raye," the gold one adds.

"And I'm Maye," the red bat says.

"An honor to serve you, Prince-Consort," Faye says. "Let's get you ready for the feast."

The bats pull the rosefinch from bed and send him back to the washroom, where the selkies scrub him down in record time—with only one offer to take his place as Prince-Consort. As he stands in the steamy washroom, the bats pat him dry and rub impossibly soft cream into his body that his skin seems to drink right up. When Raye dips his hands down to grip the swell of finch's ass to hold him open, the finch jerks out of his grip, heart in his throat.

"I thought you said no touching," the finch blurts out.

Raye and Maye exchange looks.

"Just a little oil," Maye says.

"Prepping you for the Prince," Raye explains, shrugging his shoulders.

The finch sputters, red-faced, "He can do that himself if he must!"

"I see how he got his name," Maye whispers to Raye as she puts the oil back onto the shelves lining the wall of the washroom. "I didn't think someone with his color could turn so red."

"Angels really are special," Raye responds with a smirk, and the two bats snicker.

Mercifully, they let him leave un-oiled. With a robe around his shoulders, the bats dry and treat the finch's hair, bringing volume and luster to every wave and curl that spills down his back. They press things into his face, softening his cheeks and painting his eyelids and lips. When Maye tries to line his eyes in black ink, the finch twitches away from the tip of the pencil. Raye holds his head in place just so Maye can finish.

"Don't touch your eyes or I'll rip them out," Maye says as she shoves the pencil into a pouch at her hip. "I worked hard for that."

Raye takes the finch's hand and pulls him out of the dining room chair and into the Night Prince's bedroom to stand in front of a floor length mirror. Faye turns on the brightest light in the room—a lamp that seems to hold a tiny full moon inside—and the rosefinch sees what they've done to him.

His eyes pop open and he grabs the edges of the mirror to look closer. "You've used demon magic."

The bats cackle behind him.

"Oh, please," Faye pries his hands off the mirror. "It's called makeup, little bird. It's not evil."

The finch gawks at how a few well-placed bits of paint can turn his face into something sultry. From the black lines around his eyes to the slight, silvery blush across his cheekbones, to the black stain over his lips, he looks inviting and untouchable all at once.

"We've never done up an angel before," Raye says, fluffing up the rosefinch's hair. "Kind of intimidating."

"Well, we already know the Prince likes him, so it's not like he needs to be impressed," Maye says, head cocked to the side as she studies the finch.

"It's because the Prince likes him that we need to be sure he looks good," Faye says, arms crossed. "Otherwise, we'll be accused of making him look ugly on purpose."

"Oh, shit..." Maye jumps forward, turning the finch toward her so she can use her nail to scrape off the slightest speck of misplaced shimmer. "You should have said that first."

Faye grins. "Get the dress on him already. We're running out of time."

The three of them help the finch step into his dress, finishing with a pair of silver sandals. The dress almost looks like the kind of robes he used to wear before he lost his wings, a familiar cut around his neck and looseness of the fabric over his chest, but this cuts tight around his waist, emphasizing the slight swell of his hips, and there is no extra modesty fabric fastened over his chest or between his wings. One quick spin, and most of the finch's body is on display.

Taking the finch's arm gently around theirs, Faye guides him out of the bedroom, past the dining room, through the sitting room, and back out into the main hall of the Night Palace. Heart pounding, the rosefinch sees a handful of other demons prowling through the halls. An owl-winged man drops into a bow as Faye and the finch pass him by, the tufts of his ears swaying gently when he rises back up. The finch burns with the open air on his scars.

"Arvel, is His Highness in the moon pool?" Faye asks.

"Yes, he's just about finished," Arvel replies. He turns his gray eyes onto the finch, sweeping the finch's hand into his and bringing it to his lips. "An honor to serve you, Prince-Consort."

The rosefinch erupts into a fierce blush.

Arvel smiles, a few deep lines springing up around his mouth. "I am the Night Prince's adviser. I look forward to learning more about the angel who saved our Prince."

"I'm not a..." The rosefinch clears his throat, face burning as he drops his gaze to the dark stone floor. "I'm no longer an angel."

Arvel gives the finch a pitying glance. "I meant no offense, Prince-Consort. Only gratitude."

"Alright, we gotta get a move on," Faye says and squeezes the finch's hip.

She directs the finch to the room right down the hall that had given him such a strange feeling when he'd first seen it. Now, there are two half-wolf demons guarding the outside of the door, and the finch can see the Pale Prince of Night basking in a pool of water.

The large room is dotted with a circle of engraved pillars that rise out of a layer of dark water. The Night Prince's legs are tented out of the surface, his head resting on the lip of stone behind him, long arms propped up on either side. His skin practically glows, a sliver of pure moonlight carved into this stone basin. The expression on his face is one of contentment, like nothing could ever hurt him. When the Prince stretches his arms out, back arching, like he's waking up from the most satisfying nap, he is a beautiful creature that does not belong in this world of demons.

He looks human.

New heat creeps back into the rosefinch's cheeks and he turns away.

"Is that you, my little rosefinch?"

The finch startles at the finger under his chin, the Night Prince suddenly standing beside him with a pleased smile.

"How beautiful," the Night Prince purrs.

The finch shivers at the desire thick in the Prince's voice.

With a deep breath, the Night Prince straightens up to his full height, now donning a long black skirt, cut high on both sides to show his statuesque legs. Most of his chest and arms are bare, except for shiny black bands tightly fitted around his biceps and wrists and neck. He is covered in silver and black jewelry, in his ears, and around his neck, connecting his fingers to his wrist, his hips to his thighs. Every one of his movements carries the cheery jingle of metal.

His hair gently streams around him like it's still in the water.

"Faye, when did the feast begin?" the Night Prince asks, earrings sparkling when he turns his head toward them.

Faye's wings rustle. "About an hour ago."

"An hour?" the finch gasps.

"Perfect," the Night Prince says, looping his arm around the finch's. "Off we go."

The finch clings to the Night Prince's arm as they reappear in the train station, only this time, there are other demons roaming the halls. A train car opens up, and several goat-legged demons come springing out, all of them with boxes in hand. The Night Prince waves toward a small booth in the corner of the room, and a sharp bell rings in announcement as a new car slides out from behind them and into the station.

It's much more ornate than the other cars, painted in the night's colors. It resembles a trophy more than a train, and the Prince sweeps the finch onto it without hesitation. The interior is just as ornate as the exterior, plush couches arranged around small glass tables instead of the rows of benches that were in the other car. The Prince guides the finch onto one of the cushions and graciously leaves a few inches of space between them.

The finch's head is spinning, but he steals another glance at the Night Prince, brighter than he's ever been.

"That moon pool," the finch mumbles.

The Night Prince looks at him, expectant.

The finch swallows. "It...seems to have energized you."

The Night Prince reaches his hand out to run his fingers through the finch's silky waves of hair, not a single snag or tangle stopping his movement. "I suppose it does for me what sunlight might have done for you back in your old world."

The finch's brows lift in recognition. Of course the Night Prince would blossom under moonlight.

"While you were in the human world," the finch starts, choosing every word with care as the Night Prince's gaze sharpens against him. "Were you, perhaps, not given the proper hospitality befitting a Prince?"

The finch's heart pounds as the Night Prince considers his question with a curious furrow in his brow.

"Hm." The Prince muses. "I can hardly expect every human being on earth to know how to care for a demon. They may have forgotten a few of my meals. Maybe they weren't used to how much I eat."

He touches the finch's jaw, eyes lidded with hunger as he stares at the finch's lips.

"You should feed yourself whenever you can," the finch says back. "To make up for it. I would hate...for someone to think I could be stolen from you."

When the Prince smiles at him, the finch can see the bat's teeth in his mouth.

"Aren't you generous," he breathes the words in a rumbling voice, and for a second, the finch doesn't know if his mouth is actually changing shape into a muzzle, or if that's the adrenaline coursing through the finch's body.

The finch drops his gaze, hands braced against his thighs. "What will this feast involve?"

"Too many questions and not enough wine," the Night Prince says with a sigh. "Everyone will be oh so curious where I've been and who you are, so we'll have to cut that off at the head if we have any hope of having a good time."

The finch just nods.

"Surely you had your fair share of laborious dinners and feasts upstairs?" the Prince asks.

The finch glances at the Prince's cool gaze once more. "We had a few festivals, yes. Many fasts to break. But never in excess. And we didn't wear makeup."

The Night Prince laughs, and the soft sound chases down the finch's spine. "Yes, of course. Heaven forbid you take pleasure in your body, or the gazes of others."

The finch opens his mouth to say *peace with oneself does not require ornamentation*, but he can't bring himself to speak the words given to him by those who sent him here.

Instead, he says, "Filth should be washed away, not reveled in."

"Aren't you precious," the Prince says, resting his cool fingertips on the finch's naked back, right between his scars.

The windows outside let in a violently bright orange light as they float further from the Night Palace. The ground beneath them is no longer beautiful open fields, but jagged rock and rivers of magma. The finch can hardly stand to look at the bright, bubbling liquid.

When the Night Prince sweeps his fingers down the finch's flank, the finch straightens up, heat in his face, goosebumps rippling down his skin.

"Tonight will be the first step in making you mine," the Prince says. "You will be the object of much jealousy and desire. We'll need to work together to make sure you become a proper denizen of the Night Court. My sweet sister Aurelius, the Hungry Prince, she won't take you. She loves me too much. But my dear brother Ward, I'm afraid he loves me just enough to try. I can't speak for the rest of them. I will warn you now. Don't believe anything my sibling Iris tells you."

The finch swallows. "What Court does Iris lead?"

"Iris is the False Prince. They love trickery even more than I do."

The finch's shoulders deflate, and the Night Prince laughs in his ear.

"Not to worry, little bird. I'll protect you from the demons."

His breath is warm on the finch's temple as he slips his hand around the finch's chest to play with the beads of peaked skin under his black dress. The finch holds his breath as unasked for heat swells through his legs and his hips. He can see the outline of the Night Prince's fingers under the fabric of his dress passing over his nipples.

"Is pleasure really such a steep price for your safety?" the Prince asks.

The finch's breath stutters at a sharp pinch of his flesh.

"I already agreed to your terms," he manages to say.

"Hardly," the Prince answers pitifully. "You merely rolled over. I'll have to work harder to make you admit how much you love this."

The finch tries to hold his chin up while the Night Prince shamelessly fondles his chest, keeping his thighs and hips clenched tight so he doesn't bloom and ruin his dress before they've made it to the feast. The air is warming up as they get closer to their destination, and the finch's breaths turn to soft, indignant puffs as he ignores the Prince playing with him—even when every nudge and flick and press of his skin sends a wave of vivid sensation shooting down his body. His legs want to soften, his mouth wants to open, his skin wants the Night Prince even closer, but he refuses to speak or move.

"There you are," the Prince gloats. "As rosy as when I met you."

The finch scowls, and the Prince smiles back.

When they arrive in the station of the Undying Court, the Night Prince makes a show of smoothing the finch's dress back down before offering his hand. The finch takes it, unable to trust the liquid feeling in his lower half, and the Prince tucks his finch close to his body as they exit the bustling station, the busiest, largest one by far.

"Careful now. If the others see you so dour, they'll think you're ripe for the taking."

The finch has embers in his throat as he asks, "Is every Prince of Hell so greedy? Maybe I *should* be stolen."

"Why do you think we're down here, and not up there with your lot?" the Night Prince asks, pointing at the ceiling. He looks utterly delighted by the thought. "By all means, if you intend to shop around, I won't stop you. You can't break your vow, but you could theoretically join another Prince's Court. Ward is a bit of a prude, his interest wouldn't be in you, but in taking from me. He might enjoy hurting you just to see if it would show on me as well. He isn't the Blood Prince for nothing."

The finch slowly loses his grip on his annoyance.

"Iris would love nothing more than a new toy to play with. At least they would keep you in one piece, even if it was just to drive you mad with all their games. Olive and Ivy would chew you up and spit you out into an entirely different creature. Of course..."

The Night Prince slows, catching the finch's gaze with a flash of teeth. "Even if someone did manage to take you from me, I wouldn't let you stay stolen for long. I'm afraid I've become quite smitten."

The rosefinch pouts at the Prince, sure now that he's being toyed with.

"Then I suppose I have nothing to fear," the finch says, straightening his back.

With a smile, the Prince leads them down the halls of the Undying Court. The white marble stone that makes up the bulk of the palace is full of subtle veins that sport nearly every color. It is much bigger than either the Hungry Palace or the Night Palace, massive courtyards dotted with guards in shortened warrior's skirts, half pauldrons, and a menagerie of imposing weapons at their sides. They all dip into short bows as the Night Prince passes them by, a quick gesture of respect for the eldest Prince of Hell.

The Night Prince doesn't spare a glance at any of them, just marches steadily on toward the growing sound of music and chatter and laughter.

"Should we be alone?" the finch asks in a whisper. "If someone really means to steal from you—"

"A host of guards is the sign of a frightened demon," the Night Prince says with a smile. "If I wanted to request protection, I would not be so foolish as to advertise it. I would instead quietly suggest that some of my most trusted protectors follow behind, unseen and unheard."

The rosefinch falls silent, the machinations of a much larger game slowly becoming visible to him as they enter a warm, cavernous hall. Long tables run the length of the room on either side, demons of all shapes and sizes filling every seat. The far end of the room is open to the air, the glow of the Great River beyond. A huge, jagged stone table sits in front of the river, the Undying King himself seated at the very center.

To his left, a plate is set in front of an empty, ornate chair, nothing but a single pomegranate laid out. To his right, two more empty chairs loom with plates full of food in front of them. The Hungry Prince waggles the tips of her fingers in their direction as Oma leans in beside her to fill her gold goblet. On the other side of the pomegranate plate, the Blood Prince ignores his food, scowling as he converses with a thin, scaly demon seated to his left.

The Undying King taps his fingers on the table, so obviously staring directly at the Night Prince. He wears a simple crown of bone upon his dark hair. He, too, wears warrior's clothes, softened only a little for the dinner, but most of his bulky chest and arms are bare.

A horn blares through the room, the musicians in the front of the hall pausing in their playing, and a young demon with feathers lining his chest shouts at the top of his lungs, "The Pale Prince of Night, eldest son of the Undying King, and his bond!"

Every single demon looks at them as the Night Prince strolls into the hall with the finch at his arm. The Night Prince doesn't show an ounce of surprise, but everyone stares at them with open awe and curiosity, and some less favorable expressions. The finch only tries to keep pace and not trip as they walk the full length of the room in silence, pausing only in front of the Undying King.

The Night Prince drops into a full bow, bent at the waist with his arm held out to the side. The finch startles after him, following in a stiff mimic.

"How nice of you to attend your own feast," the Undying King drawls.

The Night Prince rises back up, tugging the finch along with him. "Thank you for throwing me such a boring party."

"Will you finally deign to tell us where you've been all these years?" the King asks. "Hidden from sight even from my scouts."

"Very suspicious, if you ask me," the Blood Prince chimes in, but the King slams his fist onto the table, not once breaking eye contact with the eldest Prince.

"I did not ask you," the King says. "Silence will speak for himself."

The Night Prince has the same serene smile. "Yet again, you ask for the impossible."

"I have no patience for your bullshit," the King says, his lips curling. There is a pretty hoop of gold threaded through his nostril, rings dotting his fingers, his ears, his chest. With his neat, dark beard, he almost resembles an avenging angel, but the wild fury in his eyes is unrecognizable to the finch, and so is the deathly pallor to his skin.

"You will answer me or you will face punishment. Where have you been all this time?" the King asks.

The Night Prince straightens his shoulders. "I was in the human world investigating a very curious new cult. I fear it isn't a conversation for such polite company. May I sit and speak more quietly?"

The King narrows his eyes, and turns his gaze onto the rosefinch. "Name."

The finch startles, looking between Prince and King to try and figure out if he's supposed to answer himself or if the Night Prince will do it for him.

"He's quite a timid thing, isn't he?" The Night Prince smiles, easing his hand around the back of the finch's neck. "He wants to know the name you had upstairs."

The rosefinch goes to answer him, but fear zips up the backs of his legs as he tries and fails to say anything.

"What's wrong?" The Night Prince rubs his fingers into the muscle of the finch's neck. "Has someone cut your tongue?"

The finch turns to him, eyes wide, and the Prince gives him another toothy smile.

"Open your mouth."

The finch parts his lips, and the Night Prince wastes no time snatching the finch's tongue in his fingers to pull it into view of the King. There on the slick, pink flesh is a burning red sigil written in the characters of the angel's language. The King sits up a little higher.

"I'm sorry, my ancient languages are rusty," the Night Prince says. "Can you read what it says, father?"

The Undying King looks directly at the finch's tongue. "Those are words I can't say anymore. Can it speak at all?"

The Prince releases the finch, who covers his mouth with his hands, burning from head to toe.

The Night Prince gestures toward his father. "At least tell him your title."

The rosefinch faces the Undying King and straightens his shoulders, puffing up his chest in an attempt to salvage some of his dignity. "I am...the rosefinch." Some of his manufactured pride slips out of his grasp as he adds at half the volume, "Prince-Consort."

The Undying King reconsiders the finch with narrowed eyes.

"It seems there are many questions we won't be able to answer about my bond, but there is one thing I know for certain," the Night Prince says. "If it were not for his calling me, I would likely have been stuck in the human world for even longer still. I owe him my thanks for that, and so does anyone who is grateful to see me home again."

"Hmm." The Undying King doesn't look impressed, but he waves his hand. "Fine, come and take your seats."

Just like that, the music picks up, and the tension seems to fizzle away. The Night Prince steps up to the table so he can place the pit of a peach next to the pomegranate in front of the empty chair. Up close, the finch can see the chair is wrapped in vines, and a small flower crown sits on the bare cushion. The Night Prince bows to the empty chair before he slips around the table to take his place at his father's side, situating the finch in the chair between him and his sister.

The finch is almost immediately drawn into a conversation with the Hungry Prince about his clothes, the food, the wine, oh the wine. She fills his cup and insists he tastes it, and the finch can only do as she asks as the Night Prince talks to his father so quietly that he can't hear any of the words. It's nothing but a whisper of the wind at his side.

The wine is much louder. It fills his head with rushing water, and every time he tries to say he's had enough, the Hungry Prince has his cup filled to the brim yet again. The finch simply tries to ignore it as his head swims and the room begins to swirl. Quite suddenly, someone is standing in front of the rosefinch, dropping into a bow and offering their hand.

The finch looks at the Princes on either side of him for direction.

"Bond of the Night Prince," the demon across the table says, straightening back up. They have a lion's mane of hair, two triangular ears pierced with gold hoops, and a tail coiled politely around their hip. "May I have the honor of a dance?"

The finch's eyes flash. The Hungry Prince leans in to whisper to him, "This is our cousin, Novak. They are an honorable servant of the Cracked Prince. You're safe with them."

"I have to dance?" the finch whispers back.

The Hungry Prince grins at him and pushes his goblet of wine closer. "A bit more courage then?"

The finch takes a gulp before rising to unsteady feet. He stares meaningfully at the Night Prince, as if hoping to be told to stay put, but the Prince only scoops up the finch's bronze hand and presses it to his pale mouth.

"I'll be watching," he promises.

Swallowing his nerves, the finch steps around the table, muttering to himself in such quiet tones not to stumble, trip, or fall. Novak, the leonine demon, offers their hand to the finch, standing tall on feline haunches. They lead the finch onto the empty floor between the three feasting tables, and the musicians immediately change the tempo of the music into something with higher energy.

Novak gently places a claw-tipped hand on the finch's waist, twining their fingers with the other. "Don't worry, I'll lead," they promise in a hush.

"Thank you," the finch breathes back at them.

Maybe it's the wine loosening his limbs, or the finesse of his guide, but the finch finds himself swirling around the dance floor with more ease than he expected. Several other demons join them on the floor, and before he knows it, the finch is being passed from Novak to a slinky demon with velvety fur covering her chest. She swirls the finch a little harder, but by then, the finch has nearly forgotten that this is some kind of public function full of the most powerful demons of Hell. He laughs when a rabbit-eared demon dips him with a grin, and his face flushes with childish excitement as a large boar-tusked demon effortlessly lifts him off his feet.

The finch has no idea how many demons he manages to dance with. It feels as though he's been passed around the entire room, danced with every kind of foot and hoof and paw, when finally, he is spun around right into the Night Prince's chest.

The rosefinch startles, hands weak as he looks up at the ethereal beauty of the Pale Prince of Night. There is no safe place to touch him, dressed as sparsely as he is, and the finch freezes up. But the Night Prince takes his waist and his hand with no hesitation. At least a dozen demons must have touched him already that night, but now the finch stumbles on the gaze of the one who has so blissfully ruined him.

Already the finch's body threatens to open with only the barest contact between them. His hips feel soft like freshly turned soil as the Night Prince presses the finch against him by the small of his back. The music shifts once more, a lower and deeper song spilling over the room like firelight. The finch burns as they circle toward the very center of the floor. One by one, the other dancers give them space, or maybe the finch is just so focused on the Night Prince that everything else feels distant.

The eldest Prince of Hell is just as beautiful in motion as he is when at rest. No angle is bad, only new. Of course, the rosefinch knows more than just the shape of his jawline or the set of his lithe shoulders, or his long, elegant limbs. The finch *knows* this full-moon Prince, and now this knowledge is being broadcast to every pair of eyes on them.

The Night Prince pulls the finch to an abrupt stop, and only then does the finch notice how poised everyone is around them. Both the demons in their seats, and the ones standing on the edges of the dance floor look about to pounce, and the finch has no idea why.

The Night Prince slides his hand up the rosefinch's back, and through his hair, brushing it away from the twin scars so everyone can see the pink gouges where wings were once ripped from him. The finch's heart squeezes in his chest as he is sure every demon is studying the marks.

Slowly, the Night Prince turns the rosefinch around, draping the finch's dark hair over his shoulder. The finch doesn't know where to look as the Night Prince smooths his hands down the finch's arms. Just as he thinks to look over his shoulder to see what the Night Prince wants from him, he feels the wet press of the Prince's tongue over his scars.

Clamping his hands over his mouth, the finch squirms, but the Prince holds him fast by the hips. Everyone is watching them, watching the Prince claim his scars. The Prince tastes each one in long, messy strokes, and the finch turns red, breathing through his own fingers at the brazen display.

With a soft sigh, the Night Prince kisses the finch's shoulder, and then the back of his neck. His movements are so quiet, so intimate, the finch feels himself breaking into a sweat as he tries to control himself. The Night Prince slips his fingers into the folds of the dress to touch the finch's thigh, and the mouth between the finch's legs begins to open.

The music is still playing, but no one dares speak a word as the Night Prince traces the finch's seam, giving an appreciative sigh at the fluid already welling up. It drips down the Prince's fingers, and the finch shudders as his legs threaten to give in. He wants to disappear, he wants the Prince to take them somewhere private, he wants to melt into a puddle in the heat of this room. He is drunk, and when the Prince plunges his fingers past the rosefinch's cock and into the tight walls of his cunt, the finch moans into his clasped hands.

"This is mine," the Night Prince says.

He whispers to the rosefinch, but every demon in the room hears his voice in the air, like lyrics to the song that the musicians relentlessly play.

All except the Undying King, who is suddenly absent from the head of the table.

The Night Prince slides his fingers along the length of the finch's sheathed cock, deeper inside him, until his touch can reach no further.

"Every inch," the Prince goes on. "Every drop."

The rosefinch leans his back against the Prince's chest to try and keep himself from falling to the ground, and pleasure bursts through his spine as the Prince rubs him from the inside, coaxing his body into full bloom. The finch grabs at the Prince behind him, desperate for something steady to hold as his mind empties of thought.

"*Poison*," the finch chokes out.

"Oh, I know," the Night Prince assures him, wicked fingers buried so deep.

The finch tries to lift one of his legs up, gasping at the brief but blistering relief before he realizes he's too heavy to keep it aloft.

"I'll get it all out of you," the Prince assures him, once again only speaking to the finch. "As soon as they all see."

The finch's eyes fly open as he remembers with a bolt of fear that they are not alone. The highest Courts of Hell have gathered to watch his shame, and his breath comes faster as panic edges into his blood. So many eyes on him, lustful and heady, eager to see an angel submit to one of them. The finch can't stand it, but still his body reacts to the Night Prince like a greedy animal.

Pulling slicked fingers from the finch's hollow, the Night Prince parts the folds of the dress so that everyone can see the fallen angel in bloom. The lips of skin have pushed open, flushed dark and shiny with fluid. The stem of the angel's cock throbs in the air, a slender thing, swollen with want.

"He is an angel no more," the Night Prince whispers to everyone in the room, threading his fingers around the finch's cock. "He has become something new. And he only opens for me."

The rosefinch tries to keep back his own gasping at the Prince teasing his slit once more for the whole room to see, when a loud *crack* cuts through the music. Everyone snaps out of their reverie, turning their gazes on the Blood Prince's imposing frame. He smacks the end of his pike onto the ground again, forcing the music to a cluttered halt. Now, without the table in the way, the rosefinch can see that his lower half is coated in fur the same warm brown as his skin, haunches ending in hooves, a whip of a tail hanging between his legs.

"I've had enough of your vulgar display."

The Night Prince tilts his head. "Ahh, little brother. Did you forget whose feast it was?"

"How could I?" Ward asks dryly. "You were late an hour, and were here barely half that time before you undressed someone. Who else could it be?"

Holding out his wet fingers, strung with the rosefinch's dew, the Night Prince smiles. "Kiss my hand, Ward, and I'll forgive this interruption."

The Blood Prince holds his ground, widening his stance in anticipation. "I don't want your forgiveness, or your toy. I want your throne."

The Night Prince lowers his hand, eyes flashing. "Ah. Father said 'no' when you asked to have it in my absence, didn't he?"

Ward's shoulders tense. "I didn't say that."

The Night Prince grins. "You asked him for the Night Palace and he gave it to Olive and Ivy instead? I couldn't come up with a better insult if I tried."

Ward's lip twitches with fury and he picks his pike up, pointing it at the Night Prince. The sharp tip of the pike is flanked by a set of bull's horns that match the ones on his head. "You're useless. You and your broken bird."

The playful look drains from the Night Prince's face, along with all the light in the room. The glow from the lamps and the distant river of magma seeps out of the air like it was never there at all. The darkness that crowds into the room is not peaceful. It's impenetrable, not a single shape visible, and the finch shivers as the Night Prince leaves his side. An emptiness suddenly closes in around him, no space to even breathe, swallowed whole by an endless void. The flightless rosefinch has been abandoned in a room full of hungry predators, and fear pours off of him, sweet as nectar.

His panicked breaths puff into the air as the finch reaches out blindly, hands trembling. "Don't leave."

His voice, too, gets swallowed up by the darkness. Something shifts in the room, a wrinkle in the black velvet of nothingness, and the finch turns toward it on instinct alone. There isn't anything to see, but he can hear the sounds of a struggle. Someone breathes hard, grunting from impact, metal scrapes on stone, and he hears the hiss of air through clenched teeth.

When light bursts back into the room, the rosefinch flinches, black spots dancing in front of his eyes. Before him, the Prince of Blood is on his knees, arms bent behind his back, face twisted in a pained snarl. The Night Prince has Ward held tight, arms bound, the Prince's huge, sinewy bat wings curled forward so he can sink jagged claws into Ward's shoulders.

"Hold out your hand," the Night Prince says to the finch.

The finch lets his breath out slowly, that bone-deep fear he felt only moments ago now leaving him cold. He swallows, slowly extending his hand toward the two brothers as blood drips down Ward's chest from where the Night Prince has him skewered.

Grabbing the back of Ward's head, the Night Prince forces his brother's lips onto the rosefinch's outstretched hand, smearing a kiss onto the finch's knuckles.

"Say what you will about me," the Night Prince tells him. "But I will not tolerate disrespect for the future Princess of the Night Court."

The rosefinch blanches at that title, lips parting in surprise. Ward huffs, breath hot against the finch's hand as his eyes carve his anger into the finch.

Leaning down, the Night Prince whispers into Ward's ear, "You may stay at my feast, if you behave."

"Fuck you." Ward grinds the words up in his teeth. "I'm going to rip your entire palace apart."

"I can't wait to see." The Night Prince pulls his claws out of Ward's shoulders, tapping the gold hoop in his brother's nose once before stepping off of his haunches so Ward can pull himself back up to his full height.

"Ridiculous..." Ward mutters, stalking off with his pike in hand.

The Night Prince takes the finch's waist once more, and the finch shivers against him as the last of the cold snap breaks.

"He'll never learn," the Prince says, sighing softly. "And now our dance is ruined."

He pouts in the direction of the Blood Prince as he stalks out of the room.

"What a show!"

They both turn to see the Hungry Prince standing at the stone table, clapping vigorously. She is the only one left at the family's head table, Oma standing dutifully at her side.

"Now it really is a feast!" Aurelius gives a gleeful shout. "More music please!"

The musicians quickly rush back into another high-energy song meant for dancing, and the demons fill the dance floor once more. A few of them approach the Night Prince, and Novak claps him on the back.

"Wouldn't be a party without the Blood Prince trying to kill someone, eh?"

The Night Prince chuckles, holding the rosefinch tight to his side. "I was almost worried he wouldn't."

Novak throws his head back and laughs. "Welcome home, Pale Prince."

The rosefinch lets his breath out, finally no more lust—sensual or bloody—hanging in the air to taunt him.

The Night Prince escorts the finch back to the stone table and into their chairs, and Aurelius grins at him, offering him a small pastry. "You did splendidly, my dear. Everyone will be talking about this."

"Is that good?" the finch asks.

Aurelius shrugs. "Why not? *Princess.*"

The finch's shoulders twitch again, and he reaches for the goblet of wine. The rest of the feast is a much duller affair as demons from the High Courts approach the Night Prince and the rosefinch to give their congratulations and well wishes and ask politely impolite questions about what an angel tastes like. The Night Prince does the talking, while the Hungry Prince feeds the finch small pastries and sips of wine until the Night Prince, mid sentence with a twiggy demon, puts his hand over the finch's goblet and it mysteriously empties off all liquid.

Aurelius pinches the rosefinch's cheek. "You are so cute."

The finch feels thick and heavy, warm and full. "Why does the Blood Prince hate the Night Prince?"

As the Night Prince talks with yet another Court demon, the finch turns his syrupy gaze onto Aurelius, who smiles cheerily back.

"Ward is jealous."

"Because the Night Prince is eldest?" the finch asks quietly.

Aurelius leans down to whisper into the finch's ear. "Once upon a time, the Blood Prince loved the Night Prince more than anyone. But after one too many dalliances, Ward realized his love would never be reciprocated the way he wanted it to be. Now, because the Night Prince won't fuck him, Ward tries to kill him instead."

The finch's eyes widen. "Oh."

Aurelius plucks a grape from her plate and presses it to the finch's lips. "Ward doesn't care how many other demons would gladly do it for him. Silly boy only wants what he can't have."

The finch shivers at the burst of sugar on his tongue as he bites into the grape.

"People really will want to kill me," the finch says, gaze drifting over the room.

"You'll be fine," Aurelius waves her hand. "As long as he likes you."

Swallowing, the finch turns to look at the Night Prince once again, his pale pink lips set in that serene smile as a scaled demon offers his loyalty to the Night Court.

Without breaking eye contact with his guest, the Night Prince lays his hand in the rosefinch's lap, fingers curling over the finch's thigh. His moonlight skin is so brazen against the black fabric of his dress, an alcohol blush breaks out over the finch's cheeks as he quickly tucks the Prince's hand between the folds of fabric, hiding those long pale fingers from sight.

The finch sits up with a smug smile, satisfied in his stealth, until the Night Prince takes the invitation to touch. Back straightening, the finch's hands clench into fists on the table as the Night Prince slides a finger into the finch's cunt.

The Night Prince sees the next handful of his guests with his middle finger nestled tight against the finch's buried cock, and the rosefinch quietly dissolves beside him in an alcohol-drenched haze. When Aurelius raises another small cake to the finch's lips, he can barely chew, moaning quietly at the rich taste filling his mouth, and the long, elegant finger softening him from inside.

"Your bird is enjoying himself," the demon on the other side of the table remarks.

The Night Prince gives the finch a fond look. "Apparently he has a taste for wine."

He curls his finger as he speaks, teasing the finch's insides, and the finch's eyelids flutter shut.

"Poor thing must be exhausted," the other demon says through a smirk.

The Night Prince agrees. "I should get him home after such a long day. Aurelius, would you be so kind as to—"

"Yes, dear, I'll enjoy the spoils of your feast for you. Go on. You won the day."

She waves them away, and that time, the Night Prince spares the rosefinch the long journey home. When the finch opens his eyes, he is already back in the Prince's bed.

"Oh." He grabs the edges of the mattress to steady himself. "She...wouldn't stop giving me wine."

The Night Prince pulls his finger free, and the finch exhales like he's full of steam.

"Yes, Aurelius will do that," the Prince says, licking the fluid from his knuckles. "She'll feed you until you burst. You have to learn to say no."

The finch looks up at his demon, not a hair out of place, nor a trace of blood in his skin. "The King. He called you Silence."

The Night Prince's gaze slides onto the finch, smooth as water. "Parents do seem to have the pesky habit of calling their children by their given names."

The finch's whole face is wine-warm, his body attempting to convince him he's off balance even while he sits there.

"It's your name," the finch summarizes dumbly.

"I have many," the Prince says, leaning down to tuck some of the finch's long hair behind his ear.

The rosefinch looks at his mouth, his long nose and pale brows, all the angles in his face.

"You bested your brother so easily," the rosefinch says.

The Night Prince rests the pad of his finger against the roundest part of the finch's bottom lip. "You fed me well."

Pupils dilating, body half-melted, the finch straightens his back, puffing up his chest. "I suppose this means that—that you have earned the right to." Frowning, he searches for the right words, flustering himself the longer it takes to find something acceptable to say, until he blurts out, "You may have me again. For defending me. As a reward."

He folds his arms tight across his chest, embarrassed at his own proposal. The Night Prince rises from the bed, stretching his arms above his head. "Forgive me, little bird. I'm quite tired from all the running around and subduing my brother. You should wash the paint from your face and retire. We could both use the rest."

The finch's mouth opens. "Oh."

The Prince turns to him with a wicked smile. "Unless you are so hopelessly consumed by your desire for me? In which case, I would have no choice."

The finch juts his chin out. "No."

When the Prince turns his body again, all of his clothing seems to melt off of him, and some of the ethereal glow and luster dulls into a more earthly presence. The Prince comes back to bed, sprawling out over the covers with his eyes closed, naked and content.

"To the bath with you," the Prince says with a wave of his hand. "You smell like a feast."

The finch jumps up, shuffling out of the room with the thought, *is this really how the night will end?*

He bathes, nearly nodding off in the perpetually warm water as the selkies gently scrub the makeup from his face. He almost thanks them for not letting him drown, but his tongue is too heavy in his head. There is a robe waiting for him next to a fresh towel, which the finch blinks at, wondering who brought it and when. Everything is so soft, and so warm, as he dries himself and slips on the robe. Too warm, really. The damn wine is still heavy in his blood, and the steamy washroom isn't helping. When the finch finally makes it back to the Night Prince's bedroom, the room is dark, and the finch has to feel his way along the wall until he can make out the very faint glow of the Prince's skin as he lays in bed.

Letting his robe fall to the floor, the finch yearns for the cool touch of moonlight to douse this fire, but he is frozen by the utter stillness of the Prince at rest. It doesn't even look like he's breathing, so very still in his sleep. The finch has the distinct skin-crawling fear that the moment he touches the bed, something will snap down tight around him.

It takes him much too long to ease his hand onto the covers, with no movement from the Prince. Slowly, stiffly, the finch crawls into bed beside the sleeping demon, his body flushed from fear and wine. The eerie lack of movement or sound keeps the finch from getting any closer, but he feels downright feverish as he traces the Prince's body with his gaze.

Even just a hand to press to the finch's cheek would make a world of difference. Every second that ticks by seems to happen at half the speed as the finch inches closer to the Prince, holding his breath so as not to make too much noise. The sound of his own limbs shuffling over the sheets is suddenly as loud as a horn blaring. The finch touches the very tip of his nose to the cap of the Night Prince's shoulder, and sighs his relief at the chill.

The finch nuzzles his face to the Prince's bicep, blessedly cool on his burning skin. The scent of pine and sea salt fills the finch's nose, and he pulls the sleeping Prince's arm against his chest. He is slipping into the ocean at night. His hips tingle and pulse as he relaxes, unresolved tension still seeking a way out of him, so the finch presses the Prince's limp hand between his legs, the bump of the Prince's knuckle catching on his seam. The finch shudders, breath catching as he cants his hips so he can try to slip the Prince's finger back inside him.

"Rude," the Prince murmurs, causing the finch's entire body to jolt in surprise. "After I offered to help?"

"I was too hot," the finch snaps, moving his hands away from his own hips. "This damned wine..."

"Just the wine?" the Prince asks, fingers skimming over the finch's thigh. "It'll leave you in a few more hours if you let yourself sleep."

The finch frowns into the darkness.

"Unless something else is bothering you?" the Prince asks.

The finch's head swims in the darkness, frustration building like rust in his joints. He pushes himself up to his hands and knees, staring down at the Prince's infuriatingly calm expression, only barely visible, but the slight curve of his mouth is burned into the finch's mind.

"You said you would get rid of it!" the finch snaps, hands bunching up the sheets beneath him. "You said you would take the poison and you never did. And the wine made it worse."

The finch recoils from his own raised voice, but the Prince slides his hands around the finch's face. Perfect cool water...

"There's a bit of a temper buried beneath all that shyness." The Prince smirks.

"No," the finch immediately says, eyes closing as he leans into the Prince's touch.

"And you certainly don't like it when I touch you," the Prince remarks, sliding his fingertips over the finch's bare throat.

"No." The finch's voice quivers, shivering from the Prince's cool fingers as he cuts through the fever.

"Right," the Prince coos, dragging his hand over the finch's chest. "A powerful angel who once brought punishment to the unworthy would certainly never enjoy getting toyed with."

The finch shakes his head, pushing his chest into the Prince's fingers as they rub at the finch's nipples.

"You must hate this," the Prince says, a sharpened edge of silver to his voice. He drops his hands to grip the finch by his hips, pulling him roughly toward the Prince's chest. His teeth loom in the dark, lining his smile. "Such torture to be wanted."

The Prince corrals the finch up higher, sending new sparks of fear down the finch's thighs as he forces the finch to spread his legs over the Prince's pale neck. For a single moment, the finch stares down at the frightening beauty of the Night Prince's smile beneath his thighs, and he is not himself. The finch looks as though he belongs there, bronze knees seated on either side of alabaster cheeks, a lively flush to his body as he earns his title once again. For a heated breath, he is not embarrassed.

When the Night Prince opens his mouth to run his tongue over the finch's softening folds of skin, all the finch's poise melts away. He clings to the dark wood of the headboard as he blooms once more under the Night Prince's greedy kiss, thighs tensing. Petals of swollen skin part and shift, exposing tender insides to the Prince. The finch leans his head on his arms, hardly able to keep himself upright as his cock pushes out of his body and right into the Prince's awaiting mouth. The Prince gives an appreciative sigh, not so different from the sound the Hungry Prince gave with every new delightful bite of food at the feast. The finch moans miserably, dew already dripping out of him.

The Night Prince sucks the poison from the finch with delirious pleasure that wracks the bird's body in great waves. The sensations from the Night Prince's closed mouth are impossible. The coil of wet tongue around the length of him is bad enough, but the finch yelps as something teases at the slit in his cock, an appendage far too thin to make sense slipping inside, creating yet more unbearable pressure. The finch's fever breaks at the wild sensation pressing in around him from everywhere, and he fills the Night Prince's throat with nectar, stars bursting in his eyes. His sweaty fingers slip down the headboard, nothing but desperate mewling left in his throat as he tries not to collapse. The weight of his own body is too much to hold up, and he sways backwards. Two hands reach out to catch him, and as the finch sinks back onto his knees, he realizes the Night Prince is no longer beneath him.

The finch lifts his head, and the Night Prince cradles his face, and then his chest, and then his thighs. The finch shivers at the hands passing over him, no direction and no source, no logic at all as the Night Prince guides the finch onto his back.

"How terrible I am," the Night Prince whispers in the finch's ear, though his tongue is somehow also between the finch's legs.

"Only a monster would enjoy this."

The Night Prince spreads the finch's thighs, replacing his tongue with the head of his cock. The rosefinch has no idea where he is, lost in the darkness, unable to see, moaning as the Night Prince finally makes good on his promise. The poison has begun to drain, flowing from his body as the Night Prince seats himself back inside the hollow between his thighs.

"You may use my name if it pleases you."

The Night Prince is all around the finch now, in the very fabric of the darkness. He touches the finch everywhere, suspending him in a moonless night. The finch shivers violently as he spills again, the shadow of the Night Prince filling every orifice on the finch's aching body.

"You come more quickly than any creature I've ever fucked."

His voice is still so sweet.

"*Silence*," the rosefinch chokes the sound out in anger, pushing his legs further apart.

The rosefinch shudders, bursts of pleasure numbing his legs, reaching blindly for something to hold. Prince Silence slips his fingers between the finch's, and kisses the twin scars on the finch's back, tasting them from end to end.

"This is mine."

Dissolving particle by particle, the finch melts as the night takes him over and over again.

THE NIGHT PRINCE AND THE ROSEFINCH INVITE YOU TO JOIN THEM AT THE NEXT FEAST...

"The human world?" Silence purrs. "That is an awfully big request for a little, wingless bird."

"It is not the humans I wish to see," the finch insists, embarrassment flickering through his belly. "It is only..."

He burns at the need in his own voice, and Silence begins to laugh. "Ooh, sweet thing. Do you miss the glow of your sun?"

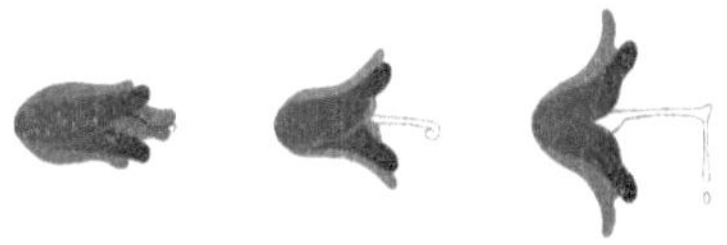

WHO'S WHO IN HELL?

The Rosefinch, Prince-Consort

A fallen angel turned flightless bird. He committed a great sin and was cast out of Heaven, so he invoked an ancient binding ritual and took a vow with a demon to share his life. The rosefinch has been severed from his old name, and cannot speak about his sin. He had not been so much as flirted with before meeting the Night Prince. When he drinks too much, he gets very impatient, though he'll deny it up and down.

The finch takes the form of a bronze-skinned young man with a dark mane of loose curls, and two deep scars on his back where his wings used to be. He's quite handsome and athletic, but the demons all think he's dainty due to his size and how quickly he blushes. Currently a resident of the Night Court!

The Pale Prince of Night; The Night Prince; Eldest Prince of Hell; Heir to the Undying Throne; (dude why do you have so many names), Silence

The first child of the King of Hell, currently the most powerful Prince of Hell, and ruler of the Night Court. He was missing for several years in the human world, and refuses to elaborate. After being pulled back to the underworld by the invocation of the binding ritual, he eagerly threw himself into the role of devoted bond to the rosefinch. He has command over the night, and is a relentless, unforgivable tease.

His greater form is that of a white bat. His standard form is that of a tall man the color of moonlight with streaming corn silk hair and a serene smile. He loves to flirt, gossip, and put his dick in troublesome holes.

The Hungry Prince, Aurelius

Currently the second most powerful Prince of Hell, and ruler of the Hungry Court. Aurelius loves all things delicious and beautiful. She's a collector, and has a bad habit of asking her sibling Princes to borrow their attendants and then conveniently forgetting to give them back. She loves all her siblings, but the Night Prince is her favorite. He spoils her.

Her greater form is that of a satyr. Her standard form is that of a round, gold-skinned woman with goat's horns. The only thing she loves as much as eating is watching other people eat. Food just tastes better with her!

The Blood Prince, Ward

Currently the third most powerful Prince of Hell, and ruler of the Blood Court. Ward is a warrior. He loves to fight and spill blood, and he's always looking for a worthy opponent. He used to admire his brother, the Night Prince, but when the Night Prince did not remain faithful in his affections, Ward decided they were enemies. Ward has not dated since, despite his many admirers. Hotheaded, stubborn, loyal, and easily flustered. (Quite prudish, in the Night Prince's words.)

His greater form is that of a raging bull. His standard form is that of a brown-skinned man with bull legs and tail.

The False Prince, Iris

Currently the fourth most powerful Prince of Hell, and ruler of the False Court. They love trickery.

The Undying King of Hell

Father to every demon, and the most powerful man in the underworld. He has a short temper, and very little patience for his children fighting. He does not approve of Silence taking a vow with a fallen angel, but can't stop it either. For some reason, mentioning Silence's mother makes him irritable.

He takes the form of a bulky man with death in his skin and thick black hair. His greater form is unknown.

 THE QUEEN OF HELL

Wife of the Undying King, and mother of Prince Silence. She isn't home right now! Surely this has nothing to do with the King's foul mood.

 OMA

A spider-demon tailor indefinitely on loan to the Hungry Court. They are a night creature originally, and are still considered part of the Night Court. They used to live in the Night Palace, until the Night Prince loaned Oma and their workshop to his sister. The Night Prince has not asked for Oma to return, and Aurelius has long since forgotten when she was supposed to end Oma's contract.

Oma is a diligent worker, unbothered by the lavish requests of either of their Courts. Though their face does not show it, they seem to enjoy tailoring for the Hungry Prince.

THE BAT SIBLINGS, FAYE, RAYE, AND MAYE

The Night Prince's most trusted attendants, the three bats help run the Night Court, and protect those who live there. They are loyal to the Night Prince, and to his consort.

THE SELKIES

The cheeky selkies who live in the Night Prince's personal washroom. No one really knows how they got in the bath water, but the Night Prince doesn't seem to mind, as long as they behave.

ARVEL

Adviser to the Night Prince. He is an older owl-demon, and denizen of the Night Court.

GLOSSARY OF TERMS

ANGEL

A creature born in Heaven, above the world of humans.

They are pious, innocent creatures that do not know sin. If an angel strays from the path of their gods and commits a sin, they get their wings plucked and they are banished from Heaven.

Angels are typically built like humans, though they run a bit smaller. Demons find angels particularly tasty. They have an intoxicating effect on weaker demons. Fallen angels are highly coveted treats in Hell. They don't typically last long. After being cast out of Heaven, a fallen angel becomes mortal.

DEMON

A creature born in Hell, beneath the world of humans. They are shameless, sinful creatures, all born from the King of Hell.

Demons have two forms, a standard form and a great form. Their standard forms are a mix of human and animal traits, usually standing a bit taller than average humans. Their great forms tend to skew more toward their animal traits, and are generally much bigger than their standard form.

Demons are aligned with particular Courts, depending on what feeds them, or what kind of creature they are. A demon can belong to several Courts at once, if they so choose. While in Hell, demons are immortal.

COURT

A grouping of demons which denotes the Prince they follow, and what kind of demon they are.

There are several fixed High Courts of Hell, and an infinite number of low courts. The High Courts are run by powerful demons like the

Night Prince, and the Hungry Prince, demons who have influence in both the human world and the underworld. Any demon can start a low court if they want to, but it won't be very powerful or influential without followers or recognition.

The High Courts have been recognized by the Undying King. The low courts have not.

Human

You know, the things that live on earth that make up stories about demons and angels.

Vow

The ritual that was established in order to give fallen angels a chance at survival in Hell. The ritual is so old, no one is really quite sure how it came to be, but no demon is able to escape its binding power.

If a fallen angel bleeds into the Great River, the demon pulled to them will become bound to the angel's life. It is said that the gravity of the fallen angel's sin corresponds to how strong their summoned demon will be.

Vows are unbreakable. If either the angel or demon dies, the other will die with them.

But just because you have a vow doesn't mean you have to be faithful.

ABOUT THE AUTHOR

DANTE, one of the first humans to be willingly allowed into the underworld as a guest of the Night Prince, spends his time detailing their many myths in pursuit of the truth at the heart of the fiction. You can find more of his work in the human world at friction-press.itch.io.

The printing of this book was made possible by the generous folks who funded it through crowdfundr in December of 2024. Thank you to every single one of you who gave money to see this created.

This physical book was edited by a nefarious, knowledgeable demon by the name of **Beleghir**. You can find more of his work in the human world at beleghir.dreamwidth.org.

The two bookend illustrations at the beginning and end of the text were drawn by a foul, resourceful demon by the name of **KMO**. You can find more of their work in the human world at kmchro.com.

The cover illustrations, as well as the mid-text illustrations, were drawn by an unspeakable, tenacious demon by the name of **SJ Miller**. You can find more of their work in the human world at sjmillerart.com.

The text and images were proofed and formatted for publishing by an abyssal, cunning demon by the name of **subvertebra**. You can find more of his work in the human world at linktr.ee/subvertebra.

The original text (published digitally on itch.io) was beta-read by a wicked, generous demon by the name of **Unrivalling**. You can find them in the human world on Bluesky at @unrivalling.bsky.social.

THANKS FOR READING!